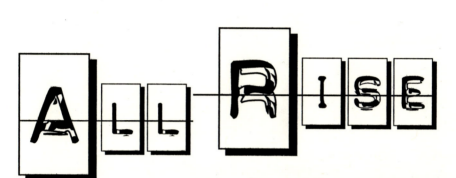

The Criminal Trial of 4 Teens

Paul Wagner

Writers Club Press
San Jose   New York   Lincoln   Shanghai

All Rise

Copyright © 2000 by **Paul H Wagner**

This book may not be reproduced or distributed, in whole or in part, in print or by any other means without the written permission of the author.

ISBN: 0-595-09151-2

Published by Writers Club Press, an imprint of iUniverse.com, Inc.

For information address:
iUniverse.com, Inc.
620 North 48th Street
Suite 201
Lincoln, NE 68504-3467
www.iuniverse.com

URL: http://www.writersclub.com

This book is dedicated to law-abiding young people everywhere. And especially to those who are innocent of any wrongdoing yet are sometimes tarnished, smeared, or branded by circumstantial evidence.

EPIGRAPH

*In the fell clutch of circumstance,
I have not winced nor cried aloud:
Under the bludgeonings of chance
My head is bloody, but unbowed.*
— W.E. Henley

ACKNOWLEDGEMENTS

Special thanks to the men and women of the Sacramento District Attorney's office—especially Asst. D.A. Chavez—and the officers and their "partners" of the K-9 Division of the Sacramento Police Department.

Also, many thanks to the sharp eyes of R.N. James, D.S. Gillin and Nicolas and Starley Wagner.

Prologue

"Freeze!" demanded the police officer. His voice trembled at the end of the word and the hand holding the gun shook noticeably. My God, thought Kelly, he's going to shoot.

Kelly froze. No movement, no thought, no breath. He just waited for it to happen. When the sound came, it was not the trigger click or exploding gunpowder, it was the unsure, uneasy voice of the man in blue.

"Put your—" The cop had to swallow. "Step away from the phone, and put your hands behind your head."

Careful not to move too quickly, Kelly did just as he was told. This cop was a very nervous individual. The process went just like a hundred arrest scenes Kelly had watched on TV. It even seemed less real than TV—until he ended up lying face down on the pavement, his wrists handcuffed behind him, his heart thudding in his chest, and his mood beginning to turn from disbelief to anger. What could he have done to cause this cop to turn jaywalking into the crime of the century? He rehashed the preceding minutes in his mind.

He'd been walking dreamily down the street thinking about that last goodbye kiss Amy had given him. He was just starting to float back to reality when he saw the pay phone outside the Taco Bell across the street. It had been only 45 minutes since he left Amy, but his impulsive heart said, "Call her!" Without thinking, he trotted across the street—carelessly, in the middle of the block. As he picked up the phone, he heard footsteps behind him. He had started to turn around and saw the quivering gun as the anxious voice said, "Freeze!"

But there must be more, he thought. And it has to be just a simple mistake.

ONE

Simple mistake?

Yes and no, Francis Kelly said to himself, sitting in the jam-packed courtroom and thinking back on his arrest. Yes, it was a mistake. But it was not simple.

And it was not over

Five months had passed since his arrest and he was about to go on trial for robbery and assault. As he watched a Chinese lady take the twelfth seat in the jury box, he wondered for the thousandth time where his guardian angel was? Throughout his entire, charmed life, someone or something had always dropped out of nowhere to flatten any bump in his path. And this was no bump. It was turning out to be more like Mount Shasta.

The room suddenly became very quiet and Kelly followed the jurors' eyes to the elevated desk of polished wood, the "bench," which dominated the room from the west end. "Juror number one," said Velma Blackwell, the African-American judge in the stately black robe, "tell us your name, the part of Sacramento in which you live, and something about yourself...just a few sentences."

As the prospective juror responded, Kelly laced and unlaced his fingers and looked at the others with him at the defendants' tables. It took three tables to seat them all. Two tables were placed end-to-end, the third joined them at right angles, forming an "L." Kelly and his attorney sat on the short leg of the "L." A balding man in his forties sat around the corner on his right. Tink Wasser's lawyer, evidently, because next to him Tink sat doodling on the yellow tablet the bailiff had left at each place. It was as if Tink was just whiling away another boring class at school, waiting for basketball practice to begin.

Beyond Wasser, Bubba Cox sat impassively, chewing on a matchstick. Next to him, his dapper attorney trimmed his fingernails with a tiny chrome clipper.

X-Ray Wade, the fiercely competitive point guard, was next. His piercing, black eyes glared at the prospective juror as if sending a curse by mental telepathy. On his right, X-Ray's attorney continually did something with his hands—tug at his necktie, smooth his jacket, adjust his shirt cuffs. His tired eyes flicked back and forth between the juror and the judge.

The assistant district attorney at a separate table spoke to the prospective juror. "Have you ever seen any of the defendants before today?"

"No," said the man.

"Do you have any relative or close personal acquaintance who is a member of the Sacramento Police Department or the Sheriff's Department?"

"No."

"Have you ever been charged with a crime?"

"No."

"Have you or a relative or close friend ever been the victim of a crime?"

Someone out in the spectator's area sneezed and the man in the jury box glanced toward the sound then quickly back to the D.A.

"Once, about three years ago," the man said, "our house was burglarized."

"I have no further questions, Your Honor," said the D.A.

"Defense counsel," said the judge. "Ms. Quake?"

Kelly turned his head to look at this Quake woman sitting next to him. She was as plain as buttermilk. At least she'd had her hair done. The mouse brown locks were still tightly curled from the permanent. Not a sign of makeup, but the natural color of her cheeks was a soft pink beneath the fine white hairs that covered her face like cobwebs. She cleared her throat and said in her nasal twang, "Do you, sir, train dogs or have any experience with dogs trained for tracking or retrieving?"

"No," the potential juror answered.

"Do you know anyone who is in the business of training dogs, or who has a trained dog for security purposes?"

"No," the man replied.

Kelly looked at his lawyer and wondered where in blazes she was going with these dog questions. What did they have to do with this case? They'd been charged with robbery, not dognapping.

He squirmed in frustration, wishing his brother was at his side instead of this oddball who showed up at the last minute. She looked like an old maid schoolteacher with that baggy print dress and cardigan sweater. And she talked through her nose, for cripe's sake. Of all the lawyers big brother Carol knew, Kelly couldn't believe this Eleanor Quake has—what did Carol say?—one of the sharpest legal minds in California, with the skill of a ferret.

Tink Wasser's lawyer began to question the prospective juror and Kelly's eyes wandered to the spectators' area on the other side of the wooden railing that divided the room. He sought his father and spotted him seated in back near the door talking in whispers to a neatly dressed African-American man in his mid-twenties. Kelly recognized the man as a law student who had worked in his father's office a couple of years ago. He used to beat Kelly every time they played one-on-one when he visited their home. The guy was not tall, but he could slam-dunk like an NBA all-star.

Dad had refused to take this situation seriously all along, saying repeatedly the district attorney's evidence was entirely circumstantial, and if it weren't for local politics the case would never come to trial. But it had.

At least he was here.

Kelly shifted his gaze to the row dominated by students from Roosevelt High. Amy was looking at him. Her blond hair was in a ponytail, and she smiled and pursed her lips. She looked great. She was great. If he hadn't had her support through this nightmare, he might have flipped out.

He smiled back, then glanced farther down the row. His big pal William Tall Bear sat with the Indian girl, Sharmin. Bear met his eyes and nodded. Bear and Amy were as different as powder and paint, and they didn't like each other, but Kelly knew he could count on them.

These guys at the defendant's table, however, were something else. Kelly ran his hand through his wavy brown hair and eyed each of them. X-ray, the leader, with his permanent scowl. Big bad Bubba with his crooked nose and chipped teeth. Curly haired Wasser, still doodling and gently fingering the faux diamond stud in his left ear lobe. Teammates, yes, but since the day they were all arrested, even Wasser, who'd been out on bail like he was, had treated him like an alien. And Bubba and X-Ray, who had been held in jail all along, barely nodded when they all met that morning for the first time since it happened. Why the chilly treatment? It didn't make sense. They were all in the same boat, victims of a series of off-the-wall circumstances.

Or could these clowns have been involved in this? They were never model citizens. They were pretty flaky. Mean and tough.

Nah, he decided, it was all a fluke—a stupid, time-wasting fluke.

Questioning of prospective jurors continued until 10:30 a.m., when the lady judge announced, "We will stop now for a fifteen-minute break. I caution all members of the jury panel not to discuss anything about this case with each other or anyone else. We will reconvene at 10:45."

Two deputy sheriffs took X-Ray and Bubba out through a door at one side of the judge's bench. Tink Wasser and his attorney began to follow the spectators clearing out through the main door at the opposite end of the room. Kelly stood up and started to head for Amy.

"Stay here," his lawyer said. "I want you to tell me all you know about Ray Wade."

"X-Ray?" said Kelly, thinking that the attorney's voice reminded him of a kazoo, like she was talking through a comb wrapped in tissue paper.

"Is that what they call him?"

Kelly nodded. "Yeah. 'Cause of the way his eyes bore into you when he stares, like he's seeing right through you. And he can find the open man on the court even when there are three guys in the way." Kelly looked over his shoulder. Amy lingered near the door watching him. He wrinkled his brow at her and shrugged. She waved sympathetically and walked out.

"Would you characterize Ray Wade as vicious?" asked Eleanor Quake.

"I don't know about vicious, but X-Ray's plenty tough. He can play in pain."

"I understand Ray—X-Ray—was captain of your basketball team. Did you help vote him into that position?"

Kelly snorted. "No way. Basketball is not a democracy at Roosevelt High," he said, repeating one of Coach Nels Hinman's favorite sayings. "The coach picked him."

"I see," she said. "We'll get to Coach Hinman in a few minutes. First, tell me about Bernard Cox."

"Everybody calls him Bubba, or the enforcer."

"Enforcer?"

"Yeah. You can see how big he is. The enforcer is the guy who crowds the opposing players. Gets rough when necessary. Takes fouls if he has to."

"You mean plays dirty—vicious?"

"Well—" Kelly gave her a sideways glance. "He did what the coach told him to."

The lawyer peered at him, her deep brown eyes unwavering. "And how about Timothy Wasser?"

"That's Tink. He was our best rebounder, and sort of the team clown. Always talking trash at the opposing players and stuff."

"Can't you tell me anything about them except what they did in basketball?"

Kelly shrugged. "Um…well, Wasser used to go with my girlfriend. But she doesn't talk about him."

"These boys were all a year ahead of you at school, is that correct?"

"Yeah, they just graduated, or were supposed to. I don't know about X-Ray and Bubba, 'cause they've been in jail since March."

"They are all over the age of eighteen, and you?"

"I'll be seventeen in November."

"I understand your mother passed away years ago, your brother Carol is back east, and your father now works out of Washington, D.C. Why are you not living in Washington with him?"

"I wanted to stay with my basketball team, so my dad and I made a deal."

"What was the deal?"

"Oh, you know, I have to make my grades, do certain chores to keep the house up, and…and I don't drive a car."

"You don't drive at all?"

"I don't drive at all."

She frowned as she chose her words. "Do you live with some other relative?"

"No," he said. "It's just me and Soo Ling."

"Soo Ling? What? A cat?"

"A fat cat," Kelly said with a laugh. "No, Soo Ling's an old friend of my dad's, sort of our 'major-domo.'"

"Ah," said Eleanor Quake, obviously relieved. She looked at the notes she had been writing. "These other boys all have nicknames. Do you have a nickname? What do they call you?"

He looked steadily into her eyes. "They call me Kelly."

She searched his eyes, then jotted another note. "All right, let's talk about Coach Hinman. He's on the list of witnesses the prosecution is going to call. Why do you suppose that is?"

"I don't know." Kelly rubbed his chin. That did seem strange. The D.A.'s job was to prove they were all guilty. Why would he want the coach to testify?

"What kind of person is Coach Hinman?"

"He's a—" Kelly almost said 'squinty-eyed racist' but thought better of it. He still had a season left to play and didn't want anything getting back to the coach. "He's sort of prejudiced, you might say."

"Prejudiced? What do you mean? He plays favorites?" Her eyes probed his.

"Not so much that."

"Wait a minute," she said. "How many African-American players are on the team?"

Kelly tilted back in his chair. "None."

Eleanor Quake made a hasty note on her pad. "I see," she said. "That's it, then."

That's what? he wondered.

The courtroom started to fill again. "We'll talk more at the lunch break," Eleanor Quake said, continuing to write on her legal pad as X-Ray and Bubba were brought back in and Judge Blackwell entered from behind the bench. As the last of the spectators settled into their seats, the stout bailiff in the sheriff's uniform, Sergeant Woznowski, tapped Kelly on the shoulder and handed him a note. "Sorry," the note read. "Duty called. I'll phone. Dad."

Kelly instinctively looked back to where his father had been sitting, but of course he was not there. He put the note into his pocket. It came as no surprise. It was all part of the price of having a father who worked for the State Department. The fact that his father had flown out from Washington for the opening day of the trial had been more of a surprise than the note.

Two

When Judge Blackwell interrupted the proceedings for the lunch break, Kelly stood up and said, "I've got to see someone now."

Eleanor Quake frowned up at him. "We need to talk."

"What about?"

"About how you happened to be at that particular pay phone where you were arrested, for one thing."

"I told you that before," he said, glancing over his shoulder. Amy was not in the courtroom.

"I want you to tell me again," Eleanor Quake said.

Kelly looked at her in frustration. He didn't like to be rude, but this woman didn't sit well with him. "Later," he said, and hurried out of the courtroom.

Bear and Sharmin were standing just outside the door near the black guy who had worked for his father. Kelly couldn't remember his name, so he just said, "Hi," and stuck out his hand.

"It's been a long time," the man said with a smile, shaking his hand.

"Hi, Francis," said Sharmin, the short Miwok girl.

Kelly acknowledged her with a nod. "Did you see where Amy went, Bear?" he asked, turning to look down the corridor. He spotted Amy nearing the elevators. Tink Wasser was just behind her.

"Gotta go." He shook his head apologetically to the black man and began to walk. "Come on, Bear," he said, breaking into a trot. He caught up with Amy and Wasser waiting by the elevators.

"Hey, girl," he said.

"Kelly," Amy said, looking happily surprised. "I thought your lawyer kept you after class again." She giggled.

"She tried," Kelly said.

"Where'd you get that weirdo, Kelly," said Wasser, "a flea market?"

Kelly ignored him. "I heard there's a cafeteria on the sixth floor, Amy."

"Let's go try it," Amy said eagerly, taking Kelly's hand.

"Sounds good to me," Wasser said.

Amy frowned at Wasser, then looked at Kelly and shrugged.

Bear and Sharmin had caught up, but stood off to the side. Just then one of the four elevator doors opened, but the arrow above the door said it was going down. Bear led Sharmin into the elevator, saying something about parking meters. Before Kelly could react, the doors closed and the elevator next to it opened, its arrow flashing up.

"All aboard!" called Wasser. Amy giggled as she pulled Kelly after her into the elevator. Wasser jumped in with them.

* * *

Back in the courtroom after lunch, Eleanor Quake took her seat next to Kelly and said abruptly, "I saw you in the cafeteria. Stay away from Wasser. I don't want the jurors seeing you with any of the other defendants and don't talk to any of them in here."

He looked at her quizzically.

"We don't want the jury thinking of you as a group—a gang," she said. "You are a nice clean cut young man. You don't look like them. You are not one of them. Understand?"

He nodded slowly, and noticed for the first time a tinge of apprehension nibbling at his mind. But we're innocent, he thought. It was all a mistake. How could any of this make any difference? This woman was really beginning to get on his nerves.

"Who was that girl?" said Eleanor Quake.

The attorney's nasal voice made the question sound like an accusation. "Just a girl from school," he said. And none of your dang business, he added to himself.

THREE

The process of selecting the jury slogged on. Candidate after candidate was asked the same questions, including Eleanor Quake's strange queries about training dogs. Kelly could feel the anger building in him again. It was all so stupid. When the judge announced the mid-afternoon break, he said quickly to Eleanor Quake, "I've got to go to the restroom." He left the table without looking back and hurried into the hall. Amy was nowhere to be seen. He paced briefly in frustration, then remembered he had noticed a pay phone at the end by the stairwell.

He punched in the long-distance number of his brother's law office and hoped he would catch Carol out of court. He was in luck.

"Hi, Bud," said Carol's hearty voice through the phone. "How's it going so far? Sorry I couldn't be there. I'm up to my hairline in a huge antitrust case. Anyway, Dad was so sure they'd dismiss the charges against you. It's crazy. What does the Lady Quake say?"

"That's what I called about," said Kelly. "She's a loser, Carol. They've been picking the jury all day, and the only thing she asks them about is training dogs, for cripe's sake. She looks like a charity case, and she's got a sinus problem that makes her sound like an off-key trombone. She—"

"Hold it!" Carol said. "Wait just a minute. You can't believe how lucky you are that she even asked for your case."

"She asked for this case?"

"That's right." Carol stopped and Kelly could hear another voice in the background. "I've got to go," Carol said. "Call me when they've finished picking the jury. And pay attention to Lady Quake. Do whatever she says. Bye."

Four

"We will recess for today," Judge Blackwell announced at 4:30. She cautioned the twenty or thirty remaining people on the jury panel against discussing the case with anyone, and told everybody to return at 9:00 a.m. the next day.

Eager to join Amy, Kelly pushed back his chair.

"Let's stay right here a few minutes," said Eleanor Quake firmly.

Kelly hesitated. Do whatever she says, his brother had instructed. He had a feeling that he'd better follow that advice, at least for the time being. "Okay," he said, "I've been wanting to ask you something. Why are you quizzing all the jurors about dogs? What do you want dog lovers on the jury for?"

"I don't," she said. "Jury selection is more about keeping certain people off the jury than trying to get the right ones put on. You'll understand later." She leaned back and gazed at him. "We probably won't present a defense. We don't have to, you know. The D.A. has the burden of proof, but it never hurts to be prepared. So, in case we decide to put you on the witness stand, let's practice it. State your full name."

Kelly blew his breath out in a long sigh, made a face, and said, "Francis Lynn Kelly."

Eleanor Quake's eyes bored into him like augers. "Francis Lynn," she echoed.

"My mother wanted girls," he said with a weary shrug.

The attorney's eyelids slowly closed and reopened as if somehow entering data into a memory bank. "You are a student at Roosevelt High School?"

"Yes. I'll be starting twelfth grade next month."

"Do you know the defendants, Ray Wade, Bernard Cox, and Timothy Wasser?" She waved a hand at their empty chairs.

"Yes. We all played on the school basketball team."

"Do you know the man in the hospital who is also charged in this case, Jake Russell?"

"No."

"Did you ever socialize with Wade, Cox, or Wasser; I mean, did you hang out with any of them when you weren't at school?"

"No."

"Are you a member of their gang?"

"What gang?"

"Don't comment," she said with a frown. "Just answer."

"No, I'm not a member of any gang," he grumbled.

"That's good," she said. "A good answer, I mean. Use those words exactly."

"Okay," he said, rubbing his eyes.

Eleanor Quake looked at her notepad for a moment. "This is important," she said in her nasal voice. "The assistant district attorney is going to say that you four boys are a tight-knit bunch. His office has done a lot of digging. Are you sure there are no incidents they might have turned up where you and the others did something together besides play basketball?"

Kelly scratched his temple to show he was trying hard to remember. There had been that one time, back when he first moved up to the varsity squad and was still allowed to drive. He couldn't bring himself to spill it to this dowdy woman. There was no way the district attorney could have found out about it anyway, and it was embarrassing. It was the incident with the girl from Grogan High. He could still picture it clearly...

The plan had seemed like a sure winner. The girl was practically famous. Every other jock at school knew about her. When X-Ray proposed the scheme and Wasser and Bubba offered to help, Kelly had been a little suspicious. He was the new kid, and they were the know-it-all veterans. But they kept needling him about being the only virgin on the team, and he did believe it was time he lost it. So he finally maneuvered at the mall that Saturday night until the girl let him buy her ice cream and agreed to take a drive. Wasser had loaned his Ford to Kelly as part of the plan.

According to X-Ray, the girl favored tall, dark types—like Kelly—and wounded heroes really turned her on. X-Ray claimed he had personally scored with her after being cut up in a fight with some guys from her school.

Since the girl didn't know that Wasser, Bubba and Kelly were teammates, the plan was to fake a confrontation someplace where nobody else would see it, and give her a good scare. Kelly would come off as the hero, then he would lose it for sure, they said.

Bear, Kelly recalled, had been against the plan when he told him about it. "Deceit is not good," Bear said. "Deceit is the white man's undoing." As if Bear didn't spend half his time hanging around the mall picking up girls.

It had, in fact, been a perfect plan. Well, almost perfect.

He and the girl had cruised a while, then all at once she said, "What do they want?" She was staring past him at another car pulling alongside. "Are they friends of yours?"

Kelly followed her eyes. "Never saw either of 'em before," he lied.

From the passenger side of the other car, Tink Wasser glared back at him without a sign of recognition. He had a three-day growth of beard, a cigarette dangling from his lips, and wore a dirty A's baseball cap with the bill in back. He looked hard and tough. Kelly had almost smiled. Wasser frowned and stabbed his finger towards the side of the road, signaling him to pull over.

"Don't do it," the girl said, "I don't like the looks of this."

"Maybe they saw something wrong with my car and just want to tell me about it," said Kelly, slowing down and edging off the road. This section of the cemetery was perfect. There wasn't a person in sight.

"Don't get out!" she almost shouted.

"Relax," he said. "I can handle these guys."

The other car parked ahead of him and his two teammates got out and approached menacingly. Kelly sprang out and walked to meet them in front of the car, where she would have a clear view through the windshield. He heard her lock the doors behind him.

Wasser flipped his cigarette off to one side while Bubba pulled on a pair of gloves. He was wearing a studded leather jacket and mirrored blue sunglasses, with his hair pulled back in a ponytail and some kind of hair net holding everything down. Awesome, Kelly said to himself. They must've knocked themselves out getting dressed up for this. With his back to the girl, he winked at them, but Wasser suddenly pushed him with both hands and he fell back on the hood of the Ford. Excellent! he thought. Get right to it. They probably should've rehearsed the fight part of this but it was going great. He'd just fake a lunge at Wasser.

He pushed off the hood in a quick move toward Wasser and was met violently by Bubba's left fist coming the other way. He heard a splat like an overripe melon hitting a tile floor, and everything went sun-white for an instant.

In a daze, Kelly felt Wasser grab him by the shoulders and pull him up close so they were face-to-face. "This ought to work great," Wasser whispered. "You're bleeding." Then he punched Kelly in the stomach.

The girl was yelling her head off inside the car and started honking the horn in long blasts. Wasser shoved Kelly onto the hood again, and he and Bubba ran back to their car, jumped in, and burned out in a flurry of dust and flying gravel.

Kelly rolled over onto his stomach to look at the girl. She was getting out of the car. The growing pain in his nose made his eyes water. As she rushed to him, he pushed himself upright and saw the puddle of blood on the hood. "Ouch," he said.

The next morning, Kelly remembered, he looked in the mirror as he brushed his teeth. Even with all the adhesive tape, you could see how much his nose was swollen. The red, black, and purple under his eye was really cool. The kids at school would definitely be impressed.

When he went to return the Ford and met Bubba and Wasser at the donut shop in the mall, they were themselves again. You'd never recognize them as the gangstas of the prior evening.

"Whoa!" exclaimed Bubba, looking at Kelly's face when he walked up to their table. "I did all that?"

Kelly passed it off with a shrug. "We should've rehearsed the fight part."

Bubba and Wasser exchanged a knowing glance, and Kelly started to wonder.

"Yeah, but did it work?" said Wasser lazily. "Did she go for it?"

Kelly sat down and said, "She was all over me like a coat of paint. I thought she was going to tear my clothes off."

Wasser slammed the tabletop and looked surprised. "You son of a gun, you did lose it."

Kelly paused a second, then slowly shook his head. "It never got that far," he said. "I couldn't get my nose to stop bleeding and it was getting all over your car, so I dropped her off here at the mall and went to the Emergency Medical Center. It took over an hour. When I got back, she was gone."

Bubba said, "I'll be—" He was looking across the tables behind Kelly. "Don't turn around, Kelly," he said.

Wasser chuckled when he saw what Bubba was looking at.

"What is it?" whispered Kelly, fighting to keep from looking over his shoulder.

"It's that big, stupid Indian, Tall Bear," replied Wasser, "and your former almost lover."

"They just sat down together," said Bubba, "and are snuggling up cozy as bedbugs, like they're having their morning-after coffee."

Things had gone click in his mind then, Kelly recalled. He'd been had by his teammates, and Bear had unwittingly topped it off. After that, he never quite trusted X-Ray, Bubba, and Wasser, and avoided them outside of basketball.

Now, sitting in the empty courtroom next to Eleanor Quake, Kelly stroked the bump left on his nose. "Deceit," he muttered, "is not good."

"What's that?" she said.

"Nothing. I can't think of anything the D.A.'s office might turn up."

#

She was waiting on one of the stone benches on the lower terrace outside the courthouse. When he saw her, the frustrations of the day flew from his mind. She sat across from the circular pool watching the water spraying into the air behind the twisted iron sculptures. She had loosed her hair from the ponytail and it moved in the warm breeze. She was always doing something with her hair. Different styles, different colors. He was glad she had let it grow. It had been short like a boy's when they started dating last winter. She would have to spend hours working on it soon, he knew, because the dark roots were starting to show.

"Amy," he said, walking quickly down the steps to join her.

"Hi," she answered, smiling, and rose to give him a welcoming kiss. "I'll give you a ride home. I've got my uncle's car. We'll have to go straight to the house, though. He doesn't know I took it, and I need to have it back before he gets home from work."

"Aw, shoot," said Kelly. "I was hoping we could spend some real time together. You know," he grinned, "quality time."

She flashed a naughty smile and punched his arm. "You." She took his hand and led him toward the street. "What did your lawyer keep you after class for?" She giggled.

Six

On the morning of the second day, Kelly arrived at the courthouse an hour early at Eleanor Quake's request. She wanted to talk about things some more, she had said.

Even at this early hour he had to wait in line to pass through the metal detectors and security officers who guarded the entrance. It occurred to him as he waited that things had come to a fine state when a citizen had to go through all this just to enter a "public" building. He watched a well-dressed older man, an attorney perhaps, place a stout briefcase on the table for inspection and said to himself: I wonder if they ever actually discover any weapons or bombs? Things are seriously wrong with this whole system. Cases like his were a good example. Time and money down the drain; and how is justice being served?

As he passed through the door-like wooden frame containing the metal detectors, a shrill tone sounded. "Step back out and empty your pockets," said the security officer.

Kelly walked back and placed his house key and coins in the small wicker basket the guard offered, then passed through the wooden frame again. No tone this time. "What a system," he grumbled, retrieving his coins and key.

He crossed the marble floor to the bank of elevators in the center and pressed the up button. Almost immediately a bell tinked, announcing the arrival of a car going up. The doors glided open and he stepped in.

There were two African-American women already in the elevator car. One wore a deputy sheriff's uniform and had a pistol and a radio on her wide belt. The other was older and looked familiar, yet unfamiliar. She was a short, slim woman with graying hair in a smartly tailored Navy blue suit. An expensive-looking briefcase dangled from one arm. A book was cradled in her other hand. She was looking at him and he averted his eyes as it suddenly dawned on him. She was Judge Velma Blackwell without the robe.

He couldn't bring himself to look her in the eyes again, but felt her watching him as he glanced at the book she held. He could see only one word in the title: "Karate," it said.

What a mind-blower, he thought. Wait until I tell Amy and Bear about this!

When the elevator reached the third floor, he stood back to let the ladies off first.

"Good morning," Judge Blackwell said as she passed.

"Morning," he murmured, following them out.

As he strolled down the hall toward the courtroom, he tried to imagine the judge working out at a karate studio, wearing one of those white costumes and making funny noises like Bruce Lee. Unbelievable.

Seven

It was a boring, frustrating day in court as the seemingly endless parade of prospective jurors filed in and out of the jury box and responded to the same, stale questions from the attorneys and the judge. When it was finally over, Kelly left with Bear and Sharmin. As they stepped outside the courthouse, he scanned the steps and sidewalk hoping to see Amy, but she wasn't in sight. She'd had to go to work today instead of coming to the trial, but he secretly hoped she would be waiting when he walked outside.

The brightness of the late afternoon sun made him squint as he turned to Bear. "Want to wander over to K Street for a while?"

"Okay," Bear replied, fitting a pair of mirrored, highway patrol sunglasses to his face and pulling the brim of his tall black Stetson lower on his forehead.

"Let's find some shade," Sharmin said.

"That pedestrian tunnel that goes to Old Sacramento ought to be a little cooler," Kelly said.

"And maybe it's too hot for all those creepy homeless teens who usually hang out there," Sharmin said hopefully.

"Stupid losers," grunted Bear.

It was a vain hope, for when they got to the tunnel there were two groups of scruffy-looking teenagers loitering just inside the tunnel entrance. The nearest was a pair of African-American boys sitting together, smoking cigarettes and talking quietly to each other. Bear kicked the sandaled foot of the largest one and said, "Move on, loser."

"You a cop?" the youth replied with a sneer.

Kelly noticed Bear's fingers begin to curl slowly into huge fists at his side as he leaned forward and repeated in a low voice, "Move on."

The two boys got to their feet, glaring all the while at the big Indian, and walked up the tunnel entrance back to the mall.

Bear watched them briefly then turned back to Kelly and Sharmin. "Don't like black losers," he murmured and looked toward the other group who had been watching silently from the far side of the tunnel. They stood like frightened statues. Two blond girls and a boy. Only their fearful eyes seemed alive, anticipating they-knew-not-what. Suddenly the boy left the two girls and approached Kelly, Bear, and Sharmin. The boy was about their age, not very tall and painfully thin. Dirty khaki slacks and an oversized, faded green tank top hung on him like dust rags on a wire. His hair was a mass of long black, greasy braids that bobbed lazily as he walked. And he was black.

"Hey, Kelly," he said.

For a moment Kelly was too surprised to do anything but stare. The boy seemed vaguely familiar.

"It's me, IQ," the boy said with a limp smile.

"Magnus Reed?" exclaimed Sharmin. "Look at you. What are you doing, hanging around with these street people?"

"These people are my family," the boy responded, glancing briefly at Sharmin.

"I can't believe it's you, IQ," Kelly said. "What…why are you living like this?"

"Hey, man. I'm free." The boy locked eyes with Kelly. "No rules, no restrictions, no—" He waved two fingers on each hand, like quote marks. "authority figures stomping on my dreams. I dooz what I choose."

"I knew you were an independent sort—like me," Kelly said. "But, this is extreme, man. How long you been living on the streets?"

The boy shrugged. "Since my cousin's stepfather kicked me out a couple of months ago; right after that hassle at school."

Kelly remembered that a teacher had found marijuana in IQ's locker and he had been suspended. "You were living with your cousin?"

"Yeah, since my mom went away last winter. One day she just left, man. Nobody knows where she is." For a microsecond the boy's eyes clouded, then cleared as he said, "I've been arrested twice, and they tried to put me in a foster home, but out here I am in control. This—" He stretched out his arms and looked upwards. "This is real independence." His eyes returned to Kelly as he lowered his arms. "You ought to give it a try, man."

"No thanks," responded Kelly. "I've never been able to solve a problem by running away from it."

For a few seconds IQ stood silently, then he punched Kelly's arm softly. "Speaking of problems, I heard you got busted for trashing a store and beating up some brothers."

Kelly shook his head. "That's all a stupid mistake. I didn't do it."

The boy stared for another silent moment. "I didn't think so. It didn't sound like your style. I can believe it about those other jocks, though."

Kelly shrugged his shoulders and changed the subject. "How do you make it? Do you have a job?"

"I flipped burgers for a week once; but there's no reason. We can get a free meal every day at the Mission. And clothes when we need 'em."

"Where do you sleep," asked Sharmin, eyeing the two white girls waiting in the background.

"Here and there," said IQ. "There's an abandoned house on C street we've been using lately, but we're thinking of setting up camp on the river bank with some other kids."

Kelly studied the thin boy. He'd been called IQ at school because someone said he had tested at the near-genius level, and he seemed able to learn or do almost anything quickly. He wrote music, poetry; and painted murals where others scratched graffiti.

"Where are you headed with all this?" Sharmin asked, waving her hand at the surrounding street scene. "Aren't you going to finish school and go on to college? You could get a scholarship. Be anything you want to be."

"You think so?" IQ seemed to be pondering what she had said as he glanced over his shoulder at the two blond girls. "Well—" He turned back to Kelly. "Maybe I'll go make up with my cousin's stepfather and give it another shot." His eyes flicked to Bear then back to Kelly. "Listen…um . . could you spare a dollar for bus fare so I could go back out to my cousin's?"

Kelly made an apologetic face. "Sorry, man. I think I spent all I had with me today for lunch." He looked to Bear. "You—"

"No," Bear said brusquely.

"Wait," said Kelly, groping in his pocket. "Here's some change. It's all I've got. Maybe it'll help." He handed IQ the coins.

"Thanks, man," IQ said. "Be seeing ya." He went back to the two blond girls and the three of them walked on through the tunnel.

"You shouldn't have given him anything," grumbled Bear.

"What a waste of talent," Sharmin said. "Why didn't you try to talk some sense into him, Francis? He seemed to listen to you."

"It's his life," Kelly said. "None of my business."

Later, as they drove across the American River Bridge, Bear suddenly slowed his pickup. "There's your carfare," he said, indicating with a jerk of his head. Kelly looked. IQ and the two girls were sitting on the riverbank, passing a newly-opened wine bottle back and forth.

"What a waste," repeated Sharmin.

IGHT

Two more days dragged by as the attorneys and Judge Blackwell questioned prospective jurors. Kelly was appalled at the amount of time being wasted. This case should never have come to trial in the first place. Everyone knew that. No wonder the American justice system was under attack.

Amy had not made it to court after the first day because of her summer job at the YMCA. He'd only been able to catch her once by phone. She had been warm and encouraging, but he missed her terribly.

At least he had Bear to chat with during the breaks, when he could get away from his lawyer, Eleanor Quake. Sharmin always tagged along with Bear, which Kelly didn't understand. Bear was an insatiable ladies' man, and his size and rugged good looks appealed to most girls. But he had never mentioned that Sharmin was anything special to him.

"Let's have lunch outside today," suggested Bear as the three left the courtroom at noon on the fourth day. "One of those catering trucks stops down the street where they're building the new jail."

"Well, okay," said Kelly, "but that's as close to the new jail as I ever want to get."

"Um," Bear responded with a look of understanding.

They took the elevator down and moved along with the crowd past the metal detectors and security guards at the courthouse entrance. Summer was at its fullest, and the outside air was blistering the way it usually was in Sacramento in August. It also meant that football practice would be starting soon.

"You looking forward to football?" he asked Bear.

"Not really," said Bear.

"Don't blame you. Those preseason-conditioning drills are torture in this heat. I've never regretted giving it up for basketball."

"If you hadn't played football when we were freshmen, we wouldn't be brothers," Bear said.

"That's true."

Kelly's mind drifted back to that rocky freshman year as they walked up 8th Street toward the catering truck. He and Dad and Soo Ling had moved back from Hong Kong just in time for football. Someone at school had started a rumor that his mother had been Chinese. Funny what people would believe. He hadn't bothered to deny it, and the kids treated him like an outsider and called him "Coolie" behind his back. Then came that night in the closet after their first freshman football game. He could still hear the deep resonance of Bear's voice as it rumbled: "This won't take long."

"For what?" Kelly had said.

"To smoke a cigar."

"I never smoked one before," Kelly said. "Or anything else. Smoking is stupid, like all this initiation crap." He stared at the glowing tip of the Indian's cigar in the blackness. "Anyway, it doesn't matter how long it takes. Don't you get it? Smoking these cheap cigar after all that pizza is supposed to make us violently ill. Those jerk are waiting to see us come staggering out of this closet covered with puke and retching our gut out. But they're not going to have the satisfaction, Bear. Do you get what I'm saying?"

"Um," acknowledged the Indian.

Kelly took two short puffs on his cigar. "We're not going to open that door before they do, and we're not going to get sick. Hear me? They think they can work us like puppet just because we're the new guys."

"How come you always leave S's off words that are supposed to be plural, Kelly?"

"Because I'm a singular kind of guy, Bear."

"Um," Bear grunted.

"The rest want us to be like they are, a bunch of mindless turkeys who flap and gobble every time Vernon the vermin whistles."

"Vernon's plenty smart," said Bear.

"He's a grandstanding ballhog, Bear, and no smarter than we are."

"Vernon calls the plays."

"He's the quarterback. He's supposed to. That doesn't mean he knows more than we do. And he never calls any of my plays does he? Or, if he does, he fakes it to me and keeps it himself." He stopped to puff the cigar lightly. "Vermin's a jerk and they're all pinheaded turkey."

The Indian smoked silently for a moment. "The boys are just trying to have fun."

"Yeah, right," snarled Kelly. He'd been through initiations before. Anybody who thought they were fun had to be as stupid as the stunts were.

Someone pounded on the closet door. "How are you doing in there, girls?" The voice was unmistakably Vernon.

"Perfect," shouted Kelly.

"Good to hear it, Coolie," Vernon said loudly.

"It's pronounced Kelly, Vermin...you maggot." The laughter of other team members could be heard. "Call me Kelly."

There was no reply and the sounds of laughter faded. The players were probably going back to their tables in the restaurant. "Stupid," growled Kelly.

"You mad at me?" the Indian said, coughing.

"No, I'm not mad at you, Bear." Kelly looked at the luminous red sphere made by the Indian's cigar. "In fact, I uh, I want to thank you for running interference for me on that interception tonight."

"You ran good, Kelly."

"I did, didn't I?" The memory of the touchdown run flashed in Kelly's mind. It was the only time he'd gotten his hands on the ball in the entire game. He had watched the passer's eyes and darted in front of the intended receiver. The first tackler took his fake and he left him clutching air. The next two fell over each other when he cut outside, but the goal line was still 60 yards away and tacklers were moving to cut him off. Then, out of nowhere came this surprising Indian, sweeping along ahead of him like a giant wave, knocking the opposition off their feet. "I wouldn't have scored if you hadn't cleared the way, Bear. I didn't know you could run like that."

"The Bear can be quick," said the Indian. He coughed again.

"Don't smoke so fast, Bear. And don't inhale."

"Indians taught white men to smoke, Kelly."

"Maybe so, but we're not squatting by a teepee on the windswept prairie. Just take a couple of short puffs once in a while to keep it lit."

It was useless. Bear's cigar flared brightly from a long pull. Stupid Indian, thought Kelly. Maybe if I keep him talking he won't smoke so fast. "How come you're going to this school, Bear, instead of closer to your reservation?"

"Coach Davis is half Piut. He saw me race at Pow-Wow last summer and talked me into coming up here." The cigar flared again.

"So that's why you're living with him." Kelly could imagine the trouble Coach Davis must've gone to in order to add this flying mountain to the team.

"Kelly."

"What?"

"The Bear's not feeling too good."

"I told you not to smoke so fast, you dumb—" Kelly stopped himself and changed his tone. "Sit down on the floor. The air's cleaner there." If this lummox started throwing up, he thought, feeling a hint of dizziness, he wasn't sure he could make it. He could hear Bear slide down the wall, and the cigar tip plummeted like a comet. Kelly lowered himself, folding his legs to squeeze between the sprawling Indian and the door. "You're not getting sick, Bear. You hear me? If you do, you're going to sit in it until they open the door. Those snotty punks can't make us do anything we don't want to do."

A fit of coughing shook them both. Kelly left his watery eyes closed as the coughing abated. He was mad at himself for letting Vermin maneuver him into this situation. He shouldn't have sided with the Indian when the hazing started. Should've stayed aloof, he told himself. Should've stayed the lean, mean loner without a first name. He liked that image. But he owed the Bear for that touchdown. He knew it, and Vermin knew it. He was clever, that ball-hogging braggart. When Vermin started taunting the Indian, he must've known Kelly would butt in. Now here they were, cowering in a closet full of smoke. What a way to celebrate their first game, and his first touchdown.

"How are you doing, Bear?"

There was no reply. Kelly opened his eyes at once. "Bear?" He strained his eyes and ears. The glowing cigar tip was missing, and no sound came from the Bear's direction, not even the sound of breathing.

"Bear!" Kelly coughed and his heart pounded. He groped in the dark. The big Indian was slumped over, still as a boulder.

"Don't do this to me, you stupid Indian!" shouted Kelly. "Wake up!" He coughed violently. "Wake up. I need you!" He reached for the doorknob, but the door suddenly opened. Vermin stood framed in the light as thick clouds of cigar smoke rolled out into the restaurant. "Bear's not breathing," Kelly coughed, crawling out of the closet.

In one fluid motion, the quarterback shoved Kelly aside and pulled the Indian out of the closet. "Call 911," he barked, instantly taking charge. He lifted Kelly like a straw and propelled him toward the restaurant's phone. As he stumbled to the phone, Kelly looked back. Vermin was giving Bear mouth-to-mouth resuscitation. Incredible.

One of the firemen who had showed up with oxygen tanks had lectured them all. "You boys were mighty lucky," he said. "Smoke inhalation is deadly business. There better not be a next time."

After the firemen left, Vermin said grimly, "You two shouldn't have stayed in there so long."

"It was my fault," admitted Kelly. He looked down at the Indian. "Sorry, Bear."

Bear blinked slowly. "You were right, Kelly," he said.

"About what?"

"Smoking is stupid."

Kelly smiled. "I wasn't trying to prove that." He looked down at his shoes. "It was my stubborn pride."

Bear shrugged. "Still friends?"

"We are brothers," Kelly had pledged.

Later, when they sliced their fingers and pressed them together, allowing the blood to intermingle, they became blood brothers. Kelly thought it was corny at the time, but Bear took it seriously.

Kelly smiled now as they approached the catering truck, remembering how he used to leave S's off words. He had given up football at the end of that freshman season, but this monstrous Native American was still his blood brother and friend. His only friend, he admitted to himself. And it was kind of odd, considering their different backgrounds. But they agreed on almost everything…except girls.

He didn't care much for most of the gals Bear took up with. Sharmin, with her straight black hair and big eyes, fell into that category.

Bear, on the other hand, didn't care much for tall girls like Amy who were street-wise and self-reliant. "She's too big, too tough," Bear had said. "The Bear likes 'em small, soft, and clingy."

Kelly looked up at the huge construction project ahead of them that would soon be a prison. The stark new walls of concrete and iron looked cold as Arctic tundra in spite of the August heat. What would it be like? his mind insisted on asking. He shook his head. I don't want to know. I never want to know. He turned away quickly.

Bear and Sharmin were busily inspecting the racks of food displayed on the side of the catering truck. Kelly stepped closer as Bear said, "The Bear's having tuna salad on whole wheat."

"Yep," Kelly agreed, "That looks right to me."

Sharmin made it unanimous.

The tuna salad wasn't as good as Soo Ling's, but not bad, not bad at all, thought Kelly.

NINE

Late that afternoon, twelve jurors were finally acceptable to the attorneys. Judge Blackwell excused the rest of the panel and addressed the chosen dozen and two alternates. "Each of the defendants you see here is charged with robbery, assault, assault with a deadly weapon, and violation of another's rights because of race. You will be asked to determine guilt or innocence on them, not as a group, but separately and individually for each count."

She talked to them for another five minutes, then had the court clerk swear them in.

Kelly studied their faces. Of the six women in the group, two were Asians and three were African-American. There were also two black men. Kelly had detected concern about the racial mix of the jury among the defense attorneys, who were all white. One or the other of them had managed to disqualify at least ten other blacks and several Asians and Hispanics. Even Eleanor Quake had excused a couple of them, although her focus had stayed on trained dogs, which he still didn't understand.

All of the victims in the robbery for which they were being tried had been African-American, according to the small story in the newspaper at the time, and the District Attorney was emphasizing the racial overtones to this case. It was one more thing, Kelly had argued, that should have made it obvious he couldn't have been involved. Color had never been a factor in his dealings with people. But no one seemed to hear him.

"Since it's approaching four o'clock," Judge Blackwell announced, "we will not begin hearing the opening arguments by opposing counsel at this time. In fact," she said, looking at the jury, "I have another case to finish up here tomorrow, so you will not have to report back until Monday morning at nine."

She went on to caution the jurors not to discuss the case or visit the specific part of town in which the crime had taken place.

Kelly slumped in his chair. Another delay. But at least they were finally going to get started, and all the crazy circumstances would be explained. This sick joke should be over by Monday night.

TEN

The Friday morning swimming class at the East Sacramento Branch YMCA was a pleasant change from the boring ritual of the courtroom. Kelly leaned back on the spectator's bench and squinted at the kids scattered across the shallow end of the Olympic-sized outdoor pool. Amy was demonstrating the basic floating technique to the boisterous 5-year olds, who bobbed and splashed around her. She's good with them, thought Kelly, shading his eyes with his hand. The reflection of the late morning sun on the water made the bright day seem even brighter. And it was hot again. His T-shirt already stuck to his back and the sweat on his forehead trickled into his eyes. He wiped a finger across his eyebrows, then flicked off the sweat. The sandwiches Soo Ling made for him earlier were probably going to taste soggy and his plan to surprise Amy with a nice picnic would be a bust. Oh well, at least they could be together for a while.

Amy climbed out of the pool. Tall and slender, she filled out the YMCA instructor's swimsuit perfectly. Kelly felt the yearning he always felt when he looked at her. She blew her whistle and called the kids out of the water, bringing the class to a close. He stood up and walked down to meet her.

"Hi, sweet man," she said. "What ya got in the bag?"

"Soo Ling made us some sandwiches, but—"

"Oh, great! I'm starving. Let's go into the lunchroom. It's too hot out here."

The room that served as lunchroom, conference room, classroom, and a variety of other uses was good-sized and pleasantly cool. Two other Y employees were already seated at one of the large folding tables having their lunch. They nodded at Amy and looked Kelly over thoroughly.

"Hi, guys," Amy said, then in a lower voice to Kelly, "Let's spread out over her where we can talk." She led the way to a table by the windows, away from the others.

As they settled into two metal, folding chairs, she grabbed the picnic sack from him and poured the contents onto the table. "Aren't you happy not to be in court today?"

"Am I ever!" he said. "I do want to get it over with, though. This just prolongs it." He shook his head. "I never thought it would get this far—that I would actually go on trial."

"I know it," she said, reaching out to pat his hand. "It's crazy."

For a moment she took large bites of her sandwich and chewed silently. "Have you thought about what might happen?" Her brow wrinkled slightly and her soft hazel eyes looked ready to tear.

"Only one thing can happen," he said lightly. "I'll be acquitted. I didn't do it."

"But, what if—"

"Amy, stop worrying. I am innocent until proven guilty." He stressed the word proven. "They can't prove I did something I didn't do. All they have is some goofy circumstantial stuff, and my dad, my brother—even my lame lawyer—say it's not enough."

Amy took another sandwich, unwrapped it slowly, thoughtfully. "Do you think I'll have to be a witness?"

"Nah," he said. "You're not on the D.A.'s list."

Amy started to bite into her sandwich then paused and smiled. "She's kinda cute…your lawyer. Strange, but cute."

"She's totally weird," he mumbled. "Let's change the subject. What do you want to do tonight?"

ELEVEN

Kelly tried to sleep late Saturday morning, but Soo Ling wouldn't have it. "Get up," the aged housekeeper said repeatedly. "Mow lawn before it's too hot."

The power mower wouldn't start, so Kelly had to use their ancient push mower to cut the grass. It took him an hour and a half, and left him with a blister on one hand.

Bear arrived about lunchtime. Soo Ling fed them tuna salad sandwiches and they played Ping-Pong all afternoon in the air-conditioned den. Bear won all but three games from Kelly, then each of them lost a game—and five dollars—to Soo Ling, who gave them 14 points up front. The little old man played with devastating power and without mercy.

As five o'clock approached, Bear left and Kelly showered before calling Amy. She got off work at 5:00. He called at 5:15. She wasn't home yet. He called again at 5:25.

"She probably went shopping on the way home," her uncle said.

He finally connected with her at quarter to nine and made a date to catch a movie at 10:00. He showered again, shaved, and spent fifteen minutes testing different after-shave lotions before he dropped and broke a bottle of his father's most expensive stuff.

At 9:30 he rode his bike to Amy's and they walked to the theater.

Amy wore jeans and a tight blouse that showed off her figure. Her skin was pink from all day at the pool teaching little kids how to swim. She looked so fresh and appealing, Kelly wanted to skip the movie.

"Let's go fool around in the park," he said.

"Now, now," Amy said. "Be cool. I want to see this movie."

The theater was jammed with kids, and the only seats they could get together were closer to the screen than Amy liked, so she pouted a while and Kelly got involved in the movie, one of the summer blockbusters everybody had been waiting for. When it ended, Amy said she wasn't feeling very well. Girl stuff, she said, so they went straight back to her house.

They kissed at the door until Amy thought she heard her uncle coming and went in with a final wave.

As he biked home, he told himself to look at the good side. She was gorgeous, she was smart, and she was his girl.

But it hadn't been one of his better days.

* * *

They talked on the phone for over an hour Sunday morning. Amy's uncle was having a crowd over for a barbecue starting at 4:00, and Amy said she would have to spend all day getting things ready, then play hostess all evening.

"Call me when it's over," Kelly said, "and I'll come help you clean up and then we can go out."

"Thanks for offering, sugar man," Amy said, "but this thing will probably go on 'til two or three a.m. I'll be wiped out. And you have to be in court tomorrow. So, let's not. But I'll make it up to you."

The day dragged by. Then Bear came over. They washed his metallic blue Chevy pickup truck, then decided it was too hot outside, so they hung out in the den, watched videos for a couple of hours, then climbed into Bear's handsome truck and cruised the mall. They were back at the house by 6:30, bored and restless. Soo Ling fed them again and offered them a chance to win back their fivers playing Ping-Pong. They talked him into cards instead.

Kelly lost another four dollars playing poker.

Around 9:30 Bear said, "I think the Bear will go to the donut shop. Maybe pick up something sweet. Want to come, Kelly?"

Kelly grinned, knowing exactly what Bear hoped to pick up. "No thanks," he said. "The way my luck's been running this weekend I'd better just hang it up for the day. Trial starts tomorrow, remember."

"Um," Bear grunted with a nod. "See ya there."

After Bear left, Kelly tried to watch TV, tried to read, then tried to call Amy, telling himself her uncle's party might not have lasted as long as she thought it would. Her line was busy for more than an hour.

"Soo Ling," he said with a sigh, "if this weekend is an omen of things to come, I've got a feeling I'm in deep doo-doo."

Twelve

The hallway outside Dept. 314, Kelly's courtroom, was filled to overflowing when he arrived Monday morning. He recognized several of the jurors as he scanned the faces of the crowd. They looked a little uncomfortable, standing alone, waiting.

When Bailiff Woznowski opened the doors to the court, he said, "Members of the jury wait out here until the judge calls for you."

Kelly followed others inside and took his place next to Eleanor Quake at the defendants' table. She acknowledged him with a glance and started writing on her yellow tablet. X-Ray and Bubba were brought in by the deputies and took their seats. Attorney Carter Atwood held a whispered conversation with X-Ray. Wasser and Bubba exchanged words, and spectators chatted in hushed voices.

Minutes ticked by.

Kelly's eyes wandered. The judge's tall bench dominated the room. An American flag stood to the left of the bench, the state flag on the right. Floor-to-ceiling panels of light brown wood covered the walls, which were bare except for a large clock on one side and a "No Smoking" sign on the other. The courtroom was smaller than the ones Kelly remembered seeing in movies and on TV. Half of the space was given over to the judge's bench, the witness stand next to the bench, the jury box, small tables for the court clerk, the court recorder, and the bailiff, plus larger tables for the defendants and the prosecutor. A wooden railing separated that section from the spectators' seats, which were filled to capacity.

Kelly counted the spectators. There were 62, including the African-American man who had worked for his father and Bear and Sharmin, who had arrived late and just managed to squeeze into the back row.

Kelly looked at the clock on the wall and fidgeted. So much wasted time, he thought angrily. What a system.

"All rise," the bailiff said suddenly.

Everyone stood up and Judge Velma Blackwell swept in, her robe flowing behind her as she climbed the steps to her chair behind the bench. With a single, authoritative nod, she sat everyone back down, then said, "Counsel ready?"

"Yes, Your Honor," replied the attorneys.

"Seat the jury," she told the bailiff.

* * *

Assistant District Attorney Luis Sanchez stood, glanced briefly at the notes on his table, then walked closer to the jury box to begin his opening argument. He was of medium build, not very tall, with a round Latino face that was faintly pock marked, and wore a freshly pressed gabardine suit that looked new. He appeared, in every sense, to be a dedicated, professional, servant of the people. "Ladies and gentlemen, Judge Blackwell will instruct you later about the sections of the law that apply in this case. She has already told you that the defendants," Sanchez turned and pointed towards Kelly and the others, "that team of young men seated there, are innocent until they are proven guilty. That is my job. As representative of the people, your representative, I have the burden of proof. And I have the proof, as you will see." Sanchez began to pace back and forth in front of the jury as he continued. "You will hear eyewitness testimony from the actual victims of this vicious crime. You will also hear eyewitness testimony by police officers who responded when the victims called for help. You will see physical evidence that clearly ties these defendants to the crime, and hear from highly trained specialists—experts—who examined this evidence." Sanchez stopped pacing and leaned slightly toward the jurors. "We will also present to you something that is especially important. You will hear testimony that, I believe, will reveal the real motive behind this vicious thing that took place on the afternoon of March third. We will show that this was, above all else, a hate crime—cruel, violent, and despicable—motivated by the basest, most bestial intentions of racial bigotry." He stopped for emphasis, looking at each juror in turn, then began to pace again. "The defense will try to persuade you to dismiss each piece of evidence. They will seek to point out inconsistencies and raise questions about the testimony of every witness. But, as Judge Blackwell will tell you later, I'm sure, it is the summation of all the facts added together that counts. And, by the time we are through, the totality of the evidence will prove beyond a reasonable doubt that each of these men is guilty of the charges brought against him." Sanchez made eye contact with each of the jurors once more, then returned to his seat.

"He's good!" Eleanor Quake wrote on her yellow tablet for Kelly to see.

Judge Blackwell rocked forward in her chair and said, "Opening remarks for the defense. Ms Quake."

"Your Honor," she replied, "I will not address the jury at this time."

As the judge called on Tink Wasser's attorney, Kelly hastily scribbled "Why not?" on his yellow tablet, and slid the paper in front of her. She wrote a reply and pushed the paper back. "K.I.S.S." was all she had written. Kelly jotted: "Keep It Simple, Stupid?" and looked at her. She nodded and looked back to the jury.

Tink Wasser's lawyer, the balding, sun-tanned Morgan Kite, had both hands on the rail in front of the jurors, leaning casually forward as if chatting across the fence to his neighbors. Leaner and more athletic looking than the others, Kite was undoubtedly a golfer or tennis player, it seemed to Kelly. Or maybe both. "It will all come down to reasonable doubt," Kite said. "The district attorney's case is entirely circumstantial. You will hear no witness positively identify my client, Timothy Wasser, as one of the men who robbed that Circle K store on March third. No witness will tell you he actually saw Timothy in that van that was chased by the police. No evidence will be presented that proves Timothy was fleeing from the police when he was arrested outside the office building on his way to seek employment." The lawyer pushed off the rail and straightened up. "Without direct evidence, there is always a doubt. And you must find my client, Timothy Wasser, innocent."

Kite returned to the defendants' table and sat down. Judge Blackwell called Wilson W. Wilson, Bubba's counsel. "Thank you, Your Honor," he said, rising majestically. The man could've stepped right out of a store window–Thomas Payne's, Clothiers of Distinction. He was immaculate, not a strand of his gleaming white hair out of place, artfully barbered, groomed with meticulous attention to detail. There, thought Kelly, is the meaning of the word fop.

The man stood looking expectantly at the judge, smoothing his gray mustache with one finger, like a performer waiting for his cue to dance onto the stage. Judge Blackwell nodded patiently and began to quietly strike the rim of her desk with the edges of her hands, a habit, Kelly had noticed, which occupied her whenever one of the attorneys spoke at length. Karate, he thought, and tried to picture the judge demolishing a concrete block with a single blow.

"Ladies and gentlemen of the jury," said Wilson W. Wilson, walking to the jury box, "good morning." He beamed a toothy smile at them and a couple of the jury members nodded politely. "Ladies and gentlemen," he said, hooking a finger in the vest of his glen plaid suit, "my client Bernard Cox is not guilty. He is a victim of circumstances. As Mr. Kite just pointed out, the evidence you will hear is all circumstantial. Oh, a terrible crime was committed. There is no doubt about that. And we sympathize greatly with the injured citizens for the suffering they have endured. It was a terrible, terrible thing that happened. The guilty parties should be apprehended and punished." He paused, then repeated, "The guilty parties. Not Bernard Cox, who happened to be seeking employment in the area the police were searching, and who was dressed in common, everyday clothing that more or less fit the general description the police officers had." He turned toward the judge and smiled sweetly. "Her Honor will instruct you as to the legal meaning of reasonable doubt." He faced the jury again. "And I am confident you will find my client, Bernard Cox, innocent of any part in this terrible crime. Thank you very much." He walked prissily back to his seat, stroking his mustache.

Not a bad speech, thought Kelly. Not bad at all. He turned to Eleanor Quake, but she gave him no reaction.

X-Ray Wade's lawyer, Carter Atwood, rose next at the judge's signal. Kelly studied the man curiously. There was something wrong with the way he looked. It wasn't his face, which merely reflected excess with its sallow complexion and half-moons of puffy flesh beneath the weary eyes. He was medium in height, slightly plump and looked uncomfortable. He frequently jutted his chin upwards to stretch his neck or ran a finger around inside his collar, as if it was too tight. But there was something else, and Kelly fussed mentally to identify it. His arms were too short. That was it. Lawyer Atwood's suit jacket was carefully tailored to fit, but his fingertips barely reached his waist as they hung at his side. He'd never make a basketball player.

"Ladies and gentlemen," said Atwood, "as we, uh, go through this trial in the days ahead, the district attorney will attempt to persuade you that everything his witnesses tell you is a fact, but, uh, you must keep in mind that witnesses, including police officers, are just human beings like you and me. They are not video cameras, are they? Their memories can...be faulty. What they think they saw is, uh, subject to normal human bias and interpretation. The district attorney told you a few moments ago...uh, he said that he will prove that this was a hate crime. It may have been. But you will hear no witness positively identify my client, Ray Wade, as one of the perpetrators...of this crime. There will be no fact brought out to prove beyond a doubt that, uh, Ray Wade is the kind of person even capable of committing such a heinous act.

"So I ask you to please keep this always in your mind...Uh, keep in mind that a recollection is not necessarily a fact. A witness is not a camera. And Ray Wade is not guilty merely because he sits at the defendants' table. He is innocent; they are all innocent, until proof beyond a reasonable doubt is clearly established. And," he ran his finger around his collar, "and, uh, I thank you."

What a loser, Kelly thought, watching the short-armed counselor return to his seat.

Judge Blackwell spent the next ten minutes advising the jury that they were not to regard as facts what the D.A. and defense attorneys had just told them. The facts, she said, would come from the witnesses they would soon hear and the evidence presented. The Japanese woman on the jury asked if it was all right if she took notes. The judge said yes, and the bailiff distributed spiral-bound notepads to the jurors who wanted them. Judge Blackwell adjourned for the morning pit stop at precisely 10:45.

*　*　*

The law student who had worked for his father came into the men's restroom just as Kelly was leaving, and they greeted each other as old friends. He was a rather handsome young man, like the black models in catalogs of sporting goods and athletic clothing.

"This is really a circus, isn't it?" the man said with a grin. "There are almost as many of you at the defendant's table as there are on the jury."

The man's name still escaped Kelly, but he bluffed his way through the brief encounter and beat a hasty retreat. He thought it strange that the guy seemed to be interested in this trial, but he had noticed him in the courtroom every day, at one time or another, and except for Bear and Sharmin, he was the only friendly person Kelly ran into around the courthouse. He told himself he had to somehow remember the guy's name so he could really chat with him.

Thirteen

As they waited for the judge to enter and the trial to reconvene, Kelly noticed several new faces among the spectators, including a woman who sat in the front row sketching on a pad.

"Who do you suppose she is?" he asked Eleanor Quake.

"An artist from one of the newspapers, I imagine," said the attorney nasally. She reached into her briefcase. "Didn't you see the story on the front page of the *Sacramento Bee* this morning?"

Kelly shook his head as he glanced at the headline she was pointing to: HATE CRIME TRIAL BEGINS.

"Oh no," he moaned. "The front page?"

Eleanor Quake nodded. "They're going to play this one up, locally. There's been talk about Judge Blackwell being considered for a federal court. And Sanchez intends to be the next district attorney. They've both been quoted in the past as wanting to come down hard on hate crimes. That's why you're being tried as an adult." She gave Kelly a grim look. "Be extra careful what you say outside. I saw a TV newsman talking to the D.A. earlier, and other reporters are around."

District Attorney Sanchez called his first witness, a middle-aged African-American man who was sworn in by the court clerk, gave his name and address, then settled into the seat in the witness box between the judge and the jury. He wore a short-sleeved white shirt, stiffly starched and open at the collar. There was the stub of a pencil behind one ear as if he had been interrupted at work to take the witness stand.

"Are you the manager of the Circle K store at 5900 Filbert Street?"

"Yessir."

"Were you there in the store at approximately 4:30 p.m. on March third of this year?"

"Yessir, I was in the stock room taking inventory."

"Tell the jury what happened."

"I heard some kind of ruckus going on out in the store, so I went to see. Four guys wearing masks were beating on everybody."

"Would you say they were working together like a team?"

"Objection, Your Honor," Eleanor Quake said. "He's leading the witness."

"Oh," said Judge Blackwell, "I think that's a fairly routine question, Ms. Quake. Objection overruled. The witness may answer."

"I suppose you could say they were like a team." The man paused to collect his thoughts. "It was mayhem. Folks were screaming and hollering. Displays were crashing over. Stuff falling off the shelves. One of the masked guys was clubbing and kicking my clerk, Wilfred Sloan. I yelled, 'Hey!' and the guy pointed a gun at me and said, 'Get down on the floor and wait your turn.'"

"What did you do?"

"I got down like he said. Pretty soon he came over and kicked me four or five times and hit me with his gun."

"Were you knocked unconscious?"

"No, but the cut on my head took three stitches."

"What happened next?"

"I heard him yell, 'All right, we're out of here.' Then I heard them leave. I started to get up, but the one with the gun came back in and reached over the counter and took all the bills out of the change drawer."

"You saw him do that?"

"Yessir. And when he headed back for the door, I pulled my forty-five."

"You had a gun?"

"A forty-five automatic. We'd been held up so many times, I got a permit and always had my gun sticking in my belt where the junkies could see it plain."

"But this robber who had beaten and kicked you hadn't seen it?"

"I don't think so, because I was laying on my stomach after he told me to get down."

"All right. What happened next?"

"I stood up and shot at him as he went out the door, and he dropped right there in the doorway."

"Your shot hit him?"

The man nodded. "Got him along the side of his head. I stepped over him and ran out on the sidewalk and fired once at the van, but it kept going. Then I went back in and called the police."

"What time was that?"

"Four thirty-seven."

"Your Honor," Sanchez said, "as you know, defense has stipulated that the 911 operator received the call at 4:37, so we don't have to call that witness, but I would like it entered into the record, please."

"So ordered," the judge said.

Sanchez walked to the defendants' table and looked at X-Ray as he spoke to the store manager over his shoulder. "You said there were four men in masks. Can you describe them in any more detail?"

"They were all big."

"What do you mean big?"

"Tall. Over six feet. One was heavier than the others."

"What were they wearing?"

"Dark pants, gloves, and two of them had on warm-up jackets. The one with the gun, he had on a dark blue sweat jacket."

Sanchez stepped to the table in front of the court clerk. From one of three large cartons sitting there, he withdrew two jackets.

"The people wish to enter into evidence these two team warm-up jackets, Your Honor."

"Tag them 'people's exhibits numbers one and two,'" said Judge Blackwell to the clerk.

The D.A. held one of the jackets up. "For the record, exhibit number one is a well-worn Chicago Bulls jacket." He looked over at the witness. "Does this jacket appear to be one of the ones the masked men were wearing?"

"It looks like one of them," the man answered.

"And, this one, exhibit number two, would you describe it for the jury?"

"It's the Lakers jacket the other guy was wearing."

Sanchez displayed the jackets to the jury, then returned them to the evidence table.

"The van—" Sanchez stopped and rephrased his question. "How did you know the masked men who ran out of your store were in the van you shot at?"

"I saw them jump in the side door and the van took off before they even had the door closed. I saw them through the store window as I was going to the door."

"After you shot the one who came back for the money?"

"Yessir."

"You said the van sped away before they had closed the side door. Then there must have been another person waiting in the van, a driver."

"Must have been," the man agreed.

Sanchez again reached into one of the cartons. He withdrew a chrome revolver. "At this time, Your Honor, the people would enter into evidence this pistol."

"Tag it number three," Judge Blackwell told the clerk.

"Do you recognize this pistol?" Sanchez asked the witness.

"It's the one the bandit dropped when I shot him," the store manager replied. "It's got the black tape around the handle."

Sanchez showed the gun to the jury, then returned it to the evidence table. He referred to his notes for a few minutes, and Judge Blackwell whacked quietly at the edge of her desk with rigid hands.

"Let's get back to the bandits' escape," Sanchez said. "Can you describe the van that you shot at?"

"It was a white Dodge Caravan, four or five years old."

Sanchez pulled two 12 by 14 color photographs from the cartons. "This will be people's exhibit number four, Your Honor, a pair of photographs."

After the clerk tagged the photos and placed them in a plastic envelope, Sanchez showed them to the defense attorneys, then handed the envelope to the witness.

"Is this the van you shot at?"

"Yes, I believe it is, because it has the sticker in the rear window."

"You are referring to the sign that says 'RAHOWA'?"

"Yes."

"Before we continue with this witness," said Judge Blackwell, "we will take the morning break." She delivered her usual sermon to the jury about not discussing the case, then left the bench.

"Well," said Eleanor Quake nasally as the courtroom cleared, "does the witness ring true to you?" She peered steadily at Kelly.

"I guess so," he replied. "This is the first time I've heard what happened. The little story that was in the paper back then didn't tell hardly anything."

"Yes," she said, looking first into his left eye, then his right, then back to the left. "Nobody was killed, so they only gave it a paragraph at the time."

"The guy who got shot," said Kelly, "what happened to him?"

"Jake Russell? He's never regained consciousness. They've got him on a life-support system at County Hospital. You sure you never met him?"

Kelly bristled and shook his head. "I never even heard his name before this trial started. I told you." He stood up and prepared to head out of the courtroom while there was still some break time left.

"All right," she said. "This Circle K store on Filbert, have you ever been there?"

"In that part of town? Are you kidding?" he said, heading for the door.

Fourteen

As he stepped out of the courtroom into the corridor, Sharmin pushed off the opposite wall and walked over to meet him.

"Hi, Francis."

"Sharmin," he replied with a sigh, "don't call me Francis, okay?"

She nodded. "How about…Frank?"

"Never Frank," he said emphatically. "A frank is a weenie."

She grinned.

"Call me Kelly."

"But last names are so distant," Sharmin said. "Last names are used by people who don't really know you."

"Very few people do really know me, Sharmin."

"I'd like to," she said.

He let that remark pass.

"Your eyes are so blue," she said, gazing up at him, "like cornflowers."

Kelly looked away uncomfortably.

"I like the name Francis," she went on.

"It's a girl's name," he said. "My mother wanted girls."

Sharmin smiled. "She raised you to be very manly."

"She didn't raise me," he said. "She died before I was a year old." He decided to change the subject. "So where's Bear, the restroom?"

"No. He had to leave. His tribal council asked him to go with some others to a hearing the Gaming Commission is having down at the state capitol."

"Something to do with the casino on the reservation?"

Sharmin shrugged. "I don't know."

They walked to the drinking fountain as she said, "Francis…Kelly, would you go with me to a rally at the capitol Friday night? It's—"

"No," Kelly said.

She looked disappointed. "We need all the support we can muster."

"It's about your tribe, I suppose," he said, bending over for a drink at the fountain.

She nodded sadly. "We're not like Bear's people who have the new buffalo, the fancy casino that gushes money. According to the federal government, we don't even exist, you know. And we've spent hundreds of thousands of dollars over the past 15 years on the tribal recognition process. We get no federal aid, no health care, no schools, no police protection—"

Kelly held up his hand. "Save the speech, Sharmin. I read about the bum deal your people have been given. I know the Miwoks lived in Yosemite for thousands of years before the white man turned it into a national park. It's unfair. But I'm not into causes."

"Why not?" she said. "We're human beings. Why don't you get involved? Why are you such a loner?"

Kelly wished Bear hadn't started bringing her down to the courthouse. He wished he had Amy to talk to. "What other people do is their business," he said. "I don't try to change them, and I don't want them to try and change me."

 Fifteen

When the trial resumed, Kelly noticed a tall cart in the corner by the jury. A TV sat on top connected by wires to a videotape player on a lower shelf.

District Attorney Sanchez addressed the store manager in the witness box. "Do you have a video recording system for security purposes at your Circle K store?"

"Yes," answered the manager. "We have four cameras up near the ceiling that cover the entire store. They record onto a 24-hour tape which we change every morning."

Sanchez took a videocassette from his evidence box. "People's exhibit number five, Your Honor." He handed the cassette to the witness. "Is this the recording for March third of this year?"

The manager looked at the cassette. "It is."

"Objection, Your Honor," said Wasser's lawyer, Morgan Kite. "Videotape can be altered—"

"We can bring in experts to authenticate this," Sanchez replied.

"But, Your Honor—" Wilson W. Wilson began.

"Counsel approach the bench," Judge Blackwell ordered.

The defense attorneys and the D.A. gathered around the judge and argued back and forth in hushed voices. Kelly looked at each of his codefendants, but none returned his gaze. X-Ray and Bubba whispered to each other, and Wasser doodled lazily on his yellow pad.

The sidebar discussion at the judge's bench continued for nearly ten minutes. Finally the attorneys returned to their seats, and Judge Blackwell spoke to the jury. "At this time, you are going to see the portion of this tape which shows the incident the witness has already described. During your deliberation, you may watch this tape as many times as you wish. Right now, we will see it only once."

D.A. Sanchez pulled the cart from the corner and turned on the tape player. The picture, which appeared on the TV monitor, was divided into four small sections, each showing a different view. The human figures in each section were so small, Kelly wondered how the jury would be able to make out what was going on. He glanced at Eleanor Quake. She looked back and shook her head as if to say: "This is not good."

When the viewing was over, Sanchez said, "We have no further questions, Your Honor."

"Cross examination," said the judge. "Mr. Atwood, we'll let you start this time."

Attorney Carter Atwood adjusted the shirt cuffs at the end of his short arms as he approached the witness box. "Can you, um, positively identify any of the defendants as one of the robbers?"

The man glanced at Sanchez, then shook his head. "No. They were all wearing ski masks over the heads."

"You testified," said Atwood, "that, uh, your store had been held up many times, is that correct?"

"Yes."

"In the other holdups, did the robbers ever wear ski masks and, uh, point a gun at you?"

"Yes."

Carter Atwood stuck his finger into his collar for a second. "Did robbers ever strike anyone during a holdup before this?"

"Yes, a couple of times."

"So, uh, except for the fact that you shot a man—and that is certainly important—but, um, except for that, this was just another armed robbery pretty much like any other, wouldn't you say?"

"No, sir. This was different."

Carter Atwood held out his stubby arms with his palms up. "But why do you say that?"

"Well, robbery didn't seem to be the first thing on their minds," the witness said. "They almost forgot to take the money."

Sixteen

Kelly took his time leaving the courtroom when Judge Blackwell adjourned for lunch. He was trying to think of a polite way to avoid spending the next hour and a half with Sharmin. Walking slowly up the aisle to the door, he let others pass him. About half way to the door, he saw Amy coming to meet him.

"I told 'em at work I had a dentist's appointment," she said with a giggle.

Kelly hugged her with delight as others stepped around them in the aisle. Tink Wasser was among those going by. He paused and said to Amy, "Any message?"

She frowned at him, then turned to Kelly, placing herself between him and Wasser, who glanced over her at Kelly, then walked on out.

"What did he mean, 'any message?'" said Kelly.

Amy studied his face for a second. "Now, don't get upset," she said. "I went to see X-Ray yesterday."

"What?" Kelly said, perplexed. "You visited him at the jail?"

"I went to ask him—beg him—to do something to help you get out of this," she said, taking his hand and squeezing it. "I thought if he would tell the district attorney that you didn't hang out with them, and weren't with them the day of the robbery, it would get you off the hook." Her eyes pleaded with Kelly for understanding.

He looked away from her. "Oh." He turned this information over in his mind for a minute, then raised their clasped hands and patted hers. "That was sweet of you."

As they walked out of the courtroom, Sharmin saw them together and headed toward the elevators by herself.

"Well," Kelly asked Amy, "what was X-Ray's answer?"

"He said his lawyer told him not to say anything to anybody. They're not even going to present a case, a defense, to the jury. His lawyer says the district attorney has to prove that they—you—are all guilty, and the D.A. has nothing but circumstantial evidence, like you said. His lawyer told him you would all get off on reasonable doubt."

"Yeah?" said Kelly. "My lawyer says the same thing."

He wondered if Eleanor Quake was really a better attorney than X-Ray's lawyer Carter Atwood, the loser with the short arms. Neither looked smart enough to cross the street alone. "Anyway," he said, pulling Amy close and kissing her on the forehead, "thanks for trying."

SEVENTEEN

After lunch, Sergeant Woznowski, the bailiff, approached Kelly as he took his seat. Woznowski handed Kelly a note and ambled back to his table at the side of the room. "Call Carol Kelly," the note read.

Brother Carol, thought Kelly, remembering he was supposed to have called several days ago when they finished selecting the jury. He tucked the note in his pocket.

The district attorney called to the witness stand a very thin, old, African-American woman who gave her name in a deep, almost masculine voice: "Camellia Brown. I'm 82 years old." A gauze bandage covered her right eye, and she leaned forward as if unable to see Sanchez clearly. The white hair on her head was so sparse, her brown scalp showed through and her lower teeth bore the telltale stains of nicotine.

Sanchez watched the jury as he asked, "You were in the Circle K at 5900 Filbert on March third when an armed robbery took place, is that correct?"

"Suh?" The old woman cupped one hand by her ear.

Sanchez turned to her and repeated the question in a louder voice.

"Yessuh," the witness replied. "I get a quart of milk, a box of saltines, and my dip."

Sanchez moved closer to her. "Dip? Do you mean smokeless tobacco?"

"Umm-hmm." She nodded, and Kelly noticed several jurors smile.

"What happened while you were in the Circle K store?"

"What's that?" she asked, cupping her hand by her ear again.

"Tell the jury what happened," he said in a louder voice.

"Them boys came bustin' in, wearin' masks and hollerin'. But I couldn't understand 'em, so one, he comes to me, snatches my purse out a my hand, and says: 'On the floor, Aunt Jemima,' and hits me by the eye. I had to have two surgeries."

Sanchez went to his evidence cartons. "At this time, Your Honor, the people introduce into evidence this cloth purse."

The clerk tagged the purse, then Sanchez showed it to the witness. "Is this the purse taken from you on March third?"

The old woman took the item and studied it. "Yessuh, that's mine. When am I gonna get it back?"

Spectators and jury members laughed. Judge Blackwell said, "We will see that you get it back after the trial, Mrs. Brown. Continue, Mr. Sanchez."

"What had you done to provoke the masked man to attack you?"

"I done nothin'," she said. "I just standin' there."

"Did the man strike you with his fist?" Sanchez said.

"Oh, no. He hits me with a piece a iron. I had to have two surgeries." She raised her hand to the bandaged eye.

"Was it a gun the robber struck you with?"

"No. A piece a iron. Another boy, he have a gun."

"You saw a gun, did you?"

"Yes, suh. A big, shiny gun it was."

"Was the person who struck you an African-American?"

The old woman shook her head. "No black boy gonna call me Aunt Jemima and hit an old granny like that."

Wilson W. Wilson raised his hand. "Objection, Your Honor. This is conjecture by the witness."

The judge responded in a slow, measured way. "Sustained. The recorder will strike that last exchange. Would you care to rephrase, Mr. Sanchez."

The D.A. paused a second. "No, Your Honor. That will be all for Mrs. Brown."

Judge Blackwell called on Morgan Kite to begin cross-examination.

"Mrs. Brown," said Kite, "you testified the robbers were all wearing masks. Were you able to identify any of them in any way at all?"

"No, suh."

"Then you cannot say positively that any of the young men at the defendants' table was even in the Circle K at the time of the robbery, can you?"

"No, suh."

"Thank you," he said. "I have no further questions, Your Honor."

Eleanor Quake rose and walked up close to the witness. "Mrs. Brown, in your testimony you referred to the robbers as boys. If they were all wearing masks, how did you know they were boys and not adults?"

Camellia Brown smiled kindly. "I'm 82 years old. They all boys to me, Missy."

* * *

The witness on the stand was a child, an African-American boy who vibrated with fear. Poor kid, thought Kelly, he's terrified.

"Try to relax, Tyler," Judge Blackwell said softly. "This isn't going to take very long." She flashed a glare at Sanchez to be sure he got the message.

"Tell the jury your name, please," Sanchez said to the boy.

The boy responded in a voice so faint, the members of the jury all leaned forward, and Judge Blackwell said gently, "Tyler, speak louder so the folks can hear you."

"Tyler Robinson," the boy spoke up, but was still barely audible.

"How old are you, Tyler?"

"Eleven."

The spectators sat quiet as statues, straining to hear.

"Were you in the Circle K store at 5900 Filbert Street last March third at about 4:30 in the afternoon, Tyler?"

"Yes."

"Was anyone with you?"

"My sister."

"What is your sister's name?"

"Daphne."

"And how old is your sister?"

"Seven."

"What happened while you and Daphne were in the store?"

Tears filled the boy's eyes and he looked at Judge Blackwell.

"It's all right," she said. "Tell what happened."

"He hit me with a chain," Tyler said with a sob, "'cause Daphne wouldn't stop crying."

"Who hit you with a chain, Tyler?"

"The man in the mask." He looked at the defendants' table, then quickly at the floor.

"Why was Daphne crying?" Sanchez said.

"He pushed us down on the floor and said 'Stay out of the way,' and Daphne just started screaming and crying."

"Did the man in the mask hit Daphne with the chain?"

"No. I laid over her."

Sanchez turned and watched the jury as he asked, "How many times did the man hit you with the chain because Daphne wouldn't stop crying?"

"Three or four times." The boy stared at the floor in front of the witness stand, tears gone, his eyes glazed over as he remembered.

Kelly felt tears welling up in his own eyes, and he blinked hard and blew his nose.

The D.A. withdrew another photograph from his carton and had it marked into evidence. It was taken, he said, at the clinic where Tyler was treated for his injuries. He handed the photo to the jury and they each looked at it and passed it on. The two black women were visibly shaken, wiping their eyes and sniffing. The Japanese woman looked at the photo, then glared at the defendants.

When Judge Blackwell asked the defense if they wished to cross-examine, the three men avoided her eyes and declined.

"Just one or two questions, Your Honor," Eleanor Quake said. She did not approach the witness stand, but spoke calmly from her seat. "Tyler, do you see anyone in the courtroom who looks like the man who pushed you down and struck you?"

Tyler's eyes scanned across the defendants and stopped at Eleanor Quake. He shrugged his shoulders and shook his head slowly.

"The witness answered no," Judge Blackwell informed the court recorder, then said to the witness, "You have to say your answers out loud, Tyler."

"No further questions, Your Honor," Eleanor Quake said.

EIGHTEEN

Following Tyler, the store clerk, Wilfred Sloan, and two other African-American men who had been in the Circle K at the time of the robbery appeared as witnesses.

"Did you attempt to resist in any way?" Sanchez asked the second man.

The chubby man leaned forward and moved his hands up and down as he replied, like he was keeping time to music. "No, sir. When he saw the money and wallet I was holding, he held out his hand and I gave 'em right to him."

"The robber took money from you?"

"Yes, sir, my wallet, too. I'd been paid that day at Sears where I work. Mr. Sloan at the Circle K, he always cashes my paycheck for me. I was putting the money in my wallet when them boys zoomed in yelling at everybody."

"How much money did the robber take from your hand?"

The man's hands bobbed rapidly with his answer. "Two hundred twenty-eight dollars…and four dollars in my wallet."

Sanchez took an envelope from his evidence cartons and removed a wallet and a bundle of cash from the envelope. "People's exhibits numbers eight and nine," he said to the judge. "One black leather wallet and two hundred and thirty-two dollars."

Methodically questioning the three men, Sanchez brought out that each had been punched, kicked, and clubbed by the robbers. Cross-examination by defense established that none of them could positively identify any of the defendants as their attackers.

After the last witness of the day, Velma Blackwell adjourned with her usual speech to the jury and the courtroom began to clear.

"Do you want to talk about this?" Eleanor Quake said, as Kelly pushed back his chair. "That boy, Tyler…I'd like to know how you feel about—"

"Someone's waiting for me," Kelly said. "I'll come early again tomorrow."

Eleanor Quake exhaled sharply, her displeasure obvious.

Blow it out your nose, thought Kelly, turning and striding out to meet Amy.

Nineteen

It was after 10 o'clock when Kelly finally got home that night. He and Amy had stayed downtown, strolling along the K-Street Mall, looking in store windows and people watching. "Let's make a night of it," he suggested.

"Better not, sweet man," she had said. "We don't want you looking sleepy or bored in court tomorrow. Jurors notice things like that."

He could still smell her perfume on his collar as he closed the front door.

"Where you been?" demanded Soo Ling, padding hurriedly out of the den. "Call you brother. He been calling all night. I fix you dinner."

"Never mind dinner," said Kelly, heading for the phone. "I had some pizza downtown."

"Pizza?" exclaimed Soo Ling. "Pizza not food." He walked toward the kitchen shaking his head and grousing to himself.

When Carol answered the phone, Kelly, realizing it was nearly 2 a.m. in Baltimore, quickly apologized. "Sorry it's so late. I was with my girl and forgot."

"Yeah, well…" Carol sounded pissed. "You better get a handle on your priorities. I talked to Lady Quake earlier this evening. She's got a bad feeling about the way your case is going."

"I've got a bad feeling about her," Kelly said. "She thinks I'm guilty."

There was a slight pause before Carol replied. "You're wrong about that. She's told me what she thinks. She's pretty sure your ex-teammates are guilty, but as far as you're concerned…well, she's not happy with your attitude, but she knows you weren't part of this thing."

Kelly chewed on a fingernail while that information soaked in. "Carol," he said, "do you remember the name of that first-year law student that worked for Dad a couple of years ago. The one that used to come out here on weekends and play basketball?"

"You mean Charlie Lawson? Old leapin' Lawson?"

"That's it, Lawson. He's been coming to the trial, and I couldn't remember his name."

"I think Dad asked him to sit in whenever he could. What I'm asking is for you to be more cooperative with the Lady Quake."

"But, Carol," Kelly said, "she's such a lightweight."

"Listen, brother!" snapped Carol. "Let me tell you about Eleanor Quake. She and I had a class together at McGeorge Law School. I didn't know her then. Me and my wise-guy buddies had her pegged just about like you have. She was a real misfit. Old-fashioned hairdo, no-fashion clothes, always wore these klutzy hiking boots and a long skirt. Never said anything. We didn't even know her voice was so weird until everybody had to give a mock opening trial statement. When she got up there in front of everybody and began to honk like a goose, we laughed our asses off." Carol paused. "We were such jerks."

Kelly could picture the scene his brother had described. "She hasn't changed, man."

"Just let me finish," said Carol. "The professor of that class was a disgusting old snob. He told her in front of the whole class she ought to forget trial law and consider going into politics. He thought he was so cute. Then, late in the semester, he threw this challenge at the class. It was a murder trial reenacted on film—a real trial, but all the names and identifiable stuff had been changed so we couldn't find it in the law library. It ended in a hung jury. The challenge was to guess how each member of the jury voted and why. Anybody who got it right would get an A for the entire semester, no matter what their grade had been up 'til then. The smug old bastard told us he had made the offer to every class for 14 years and nobody ever got it right.

"Jordy Gleason and I even tried running it through his dad's computer, but the possible answers were in the hundreds of thousands. And we couldn't come up with the 'why' anyway."

"You're going to tell me," said Kelly. "Eleanor Quack got the answer."

"She got it," said Carol. "In ten days, she found the case and old newspaper interviews with the jurors about why they voted the way they did."

"Okay, so she's a whiz at research—"

"She can find things people don't even know are lost," Carol said. "But that's not all of it. She's got a sense like a gypsy fortune-teller. She reads people better than you read your playbook—that includes juries. She says Prosecutor Sanchez has gathered enough evidence to sink a ship, and he's putting it together piece by piece for the jury like a master craftsman." Carol's tone of voice changed. "I remember Luis Sanchez. When we were in law school, his sister got killed by a drunk driver–a wealthy, white real estate developer whose attorney plea-bargained him out of any jail time. Sanchez had almost flunked out of school before that happened, but he graduated in the upper ten percent."

Carol's voice became more concerned. "He's a zealot, brother, and it sounds like he's really got his teeth into this. I tried to call Dad, but they've sent him out of the country someplace. You quit screwing around with that girl and pay attention to what's happening. I'm going to try to get out there next week."

"Next week?" Kelly exclaimed. "It'll be over before—"

"In the meantime," Carol said, "do exactly what Lady Quake says. Exactly, hear me?"

"I hear." Kelly hung up the phone and tried to feel some of the concern his brother had communicated. But it just didn't make sense. How could they be convicted of something they hadn't done? There was no direct evidence, the lawyers had said. So what if Eleanor Quack had a bad feeling? It was probably just a gas pain. That's what she was, in his opinion, a stuffed-sinus gas pain. Any lawyer as good as Carol said she was supposed to be would've gotten him out of this before now.

Twenty

Radio newscasts on every local station played up the heat wave Tuesday morning. "A high of 109 is expected today," they said. There was no delta breeze and not a cloud in the sky. At 9:30 the air conditioning units for the third floor of the courthouse building stopped functioning.

"We'll recess for ten minutes," Judge Blackwell announced. Participants and spectators moved out into the corridor where they milled around commiserating about the heat. Kelly sat with Bear and Sharmin on one of the padded benches across from the courtroom door. Seated on the other side of Bear, on the same bench, were two uniformed police officers.

Kelly nudged Bear and whispered, "That little cop on the end is the one who arrested me." Kelly shook his head in disbelief. "He seemed a lot taller then."

Across from them, at one side of the courtroom door, prosecutor Sanchez spoke with a woman reporter who held a small tape recorder. Near the other side of the door, defense attorneys Atwood, Kite, and Wilson stood talking.

Bear looked at them and murmured to Kelly, "The white-haired one, that's Wilson W. Wilson, right?"

Kelly nodded.

"You suppose his middle initial stands for Wilson, too?" Bear said.

Kelly chuckled. "I bet it does, Bear," he said. "But I'd die before I'd ask."

Eleanor Quake clomped into view, her arms filled with a couple of binders and a stack of tablets and papers. An apple sat on the top of her load. Kelly snorted to himself. What a freak she was. His brother's reassurances had not convinced him that this frumpy misfit had all the right stuff.

"That squaw lawyer," said Bear, "you happy with her?"

Kelly started to confess his concern, but at that moment Sergeant Woznowski, the bailiff pushed open the doors to the courtroom and everybody began to file back in.

"They're working on the air-conditioning," Judge Blackwell said. "It should be operating again soon. In the meantime, we're going to try and make the best of a bad situation and continue the trial. Gentlemen on the jury and at the defendants' table may remove their jackets, if they wish. You, too, Mr. Sanchez."

She paused and the men took off their suit coats, except for Wilson W. Wilson, who shook his head with a wave and smiled bravely.

"Call your next witness," said the judge.

The police officer who had been seated next to Bear in the corridor was summoned.

His uniform was khaki, not blue, and he carried himself with the quiet assurance of experience. Sandy-haired, he had a thin, neatly trimmed mustache and a gold canine tooth that caught the light when he spoke. During the swearing-in process, Kelly studied the large diagram, which now stood on an easel next to the witness stand. It was a crudely drawn map and contained the names of Filbert Street and several cross-streets.

"Officer Cooper," said District Attorney Sanchez, "you are a member of the police department's K-9 division, is that correct?"

"Yes," Cooper said, "I've been with K-9 eight years."

"Would you describe for the jury, please, any special training you have had?"

For nine or ten minutes, Cooper told of attending programs in Sacramento and other parts of the state, including two conducted by the FBI and three put on by the Treasury Department's Narcotics Division. He went into detail about training exercises and examinations involving him and his current "partner," a German shepherd dog called Primo.

"Your Honor," said Wilson W. Wilson, raising his hand, "the defense is willing to stipulate that Sergeant Cooper is an expert in his field, if it pleases Your Honor."

"I believe it's important, Your Honor," the D.A. responded, "that we be allowed to give the jury more detail, since this kind of investigative specialty is not generally understood."

Judge Blackwell thought a moment. "Counsel approach," she said. The lawyers left their seats and held another sidebar with the judge.

After a few minutes of hushed words, the attorneys walked back to their seats, and Judge Blackwell said, "Go ahead, Mr. Sanchez."

"All right," he said. "Officer Cooper, explain to the jury, please, how your dog, Primo, is able to identify a suspect by scent."

The witness swiveled his chair to face the jury. "Of all the senses—taste, touch, sight, and so on—a dog's sense of smell is his most advanced sense. To give you an idea of how highly developed it is, there are about five million sensory receptors in a human's nasal passages. A dog has over two hundred million."

He paused a few seconds to let that register completely. "And a large part of a dog's brain is devoted to interpreting scent. When you or I go into a house where a cake is baking, we smell a cake baking. A dog smells flour, sugar, shortening—each of the individual ingredients in the cake and its proportion to the overall aroma. A human's body odor is made up of individual ingredients, also, and the specific ingredients and their share of the total are unique to each person. This odor radiates from us in millions of microscopic particles, which remain in the air and on the ground for many, many hours, depending on the weather. Primo is trained to detect a human odor, identify it, and follow it wherever it leads."

The witness swiveled his chair back to face the prosecutor.

"Thank you, Officer Cooper." Sanchez referred once again to his notes. "Now, were you on duty on March third of this year?"

"Yes."

"What was the weather like that day?"

"A lot cooler than it is today."

Everyone laughed.

Sanchez smiled and waited a moment. "Was it windy, dark, cloudy?"

"No," Cooper said, quickly back to business. "It was clear, no wind."

"Where were you at approximately 4:40 that afternoon?"

"I was in my patrol car with Primo driving east on Filbert when I heard the call on the radio about the robbery at the Circle K. The dispatcher was just giving a description of the escape vehicle when I saw a white van coming towards me about a block away. It ran a stop light at Ninth Avenue."

"What did you do?"

"I immediately made a U-turn and pursued the van with my siren and red lights on."

"Was there anything about the van you were chasing that made it easy to follow?"

"There was a sticker in the rear window with the letters R-A-H-O-W-A."

Sanchez pointed to the easel standing near Cooper. "Would you please step out and indicate on the diagram the route taken by the van?"

The females on the jury were fanning themselves with their notepads, and the defendants and attorneys filled glasses from the pitchers of ice water on their tables and drank frequently. Only Judge Blackwell and Wilson Wilson seemed unruffled by the heat.

Officer Cooper left the witness box and stood by the easel. "The van ran another stop light at Seventh Avenue," he said, pointing with his finger. "It then turned north on Quimby, then right at the next corner onto Camron street, a residential street. I followed it and closed to within two or three car lengths. The van pulled over as it got near the end of the block. It stopped just about here in front of the next-to-last house." He marked the spot on the diagram with an X. "At that point," he said, "I sent Primo out of the car and I followed him."

"What happened next?"

"Primo is trained to always go to the driver's door of a vehicle. As I followed him, the suspects jumped out of the other side of the van and ran between the houses."

"Could you see the suspects?"

"I got just a glimpse of them as they fled through a gate in the fence between the houses. It's a six-foot board fence, and they closed the gate behind them. When I got to the gate, I was unable to get it open for about four or five minutes."

Sanchez nodded. "You said you got just a glimpse of them. Can you describe what you saw?"

"I saw three white males going through the gate. The fourth must have gone through before I came around the van."

"Objection, Your Honor," said Eleanor Quake. "The witness is speculating that there was a fourth suspect."

"Sustained," said the judge.

"All right." Sanchez thought for a few seconds. "Did you see the suspects open the gate?"

"No, the gate was open and they were just going through it."

"So, the gate could have been opened by a fourth suspect who was ahead of them?"

"Yes."

"What were the suspects wearing?"

"They all had on dark trousers and light-colored sweatshirts."

"Were you able to determine anything else that would describe the suspects you saw?"

"They were tall," Cooper said, "six feet or better. One had dark hair. Another was wearing a black baseball cap, with the bill to the back."

"What did you do next?"

"I had Primo work the ground at the gate to pick up the scent, and called in my location and the description of the suspects on my handheld radio. Then Primo led me through the backyard, following the scent. On the ground next to a metal storage building located approximately here," Cooper marked the diagram, "Primo discovered a wallet shoved under some lumber."

"I now show you people's exhibit number eight," Sanchez said, taking the wallet from the evidence table and carrying it to the witness. "Can you identify this as the wallet Primo found under the lumber?"

"Yes," replied Cooper. "And, nearby, under some bushes, Primo found the Chicago warm-up jacket. Then the scent led to the back fence where the suspects jumped over. There was a gate in the corner, over here, about 30 feet from where they climbed over." Cooper pointed on the diagram. "I called Primo to me and we went through the gate. The fence separates the residential property from the driveway-parking area of this office building that faces onto Filbert Street. Right after I came through the gate, a police patrol car pulled into the driveway from Seventh Avenue and I saw three of the suspects trying to open a rear door to the office building. I ordered Primo to pursue them and he ran at them, barking. The patrol car pulled right up close to them as I approached, and when the suspects heard the dog coming and saw the black and white, they laid down on the ground. Officers Chung and Dalton got out of the car and apprehended the suspects."

"Do you see those three suspects here in the courtroom?"

"Yes. Ray Wade, Bernard Cox, and Timothy Wasser," the officer said, pointing at the defendants.

"All right," Sanchez said, checking his notes. "How much time had passed between the moment you saw the van run the first stoplight and the moment the suspects were captured?"

"It couldn't have taken more than six or seven minutes."

"What happened next?"

"I called Primo and went to look for the fourth suspect, who, I figured, must have gone into the backyard of the house on the corner." Cooper indicated the direction on the diagram. "I brought Primo to heel and walked over to the Seventh Avenue side. As I came onto the sidewalk here," he pointed on the diagram, "I spotted the suspect ahead of me. He was crossing from my side of the street over to a Taco Bell. Another black and white—"

"A police patrol car?" Sanchez said.

"Right. He was approaching from up here on Seventh. I called him on my radio, and he whipped into the Taco Bell and apprehended the suspect."

"Were you able to get a clear look at the suspect?"

"Yes, it was the defendant at the far end there, Francis Kelly."

Sanchez looked at Kelly, then looked at the jury. "Thank you, officer. Oh, one more thing." Sanchez rubbed his hands together. "You said earlier Primo is rated number one in the K-9 division."

"Yes."

"Have you and Primo been involved in the identification and apprehension of suspects other than those in this case?"

"Yes. We've been directly involved in four other arrests."

"Were those suspects brought to trial?"

"Yes."

"And what were the results?"

"All four were convictions."

"Your witness," Sanchez said to the defense attorneys.

"Ms. Quake," Judge Blackwell said.

Eleanor Quake stood up. "Officer Cooper, if Primo is rated number one in the K-9 division, does that mean he is the best?"

"Yes, it does."

"The best of all the dogs at identifying suspects by their scent?"

"That is correct. He doesn't miss."

Eleanor Quake nodded, looking at the jury. She walked to the easel next to the witness stand and pointed with her finger. "The first time you saw Francis Kelly, you were about here on Seventh Avenue, is that correct?"

"Yes, I was just coming from the driveway onto the sidewalk."

"Did your dog Primo give any indication that he was scenting a suspect?"

"No."

"He did not come to alert or anything?"

"No."

"Did you see Francis Kelly climbing over the fence to get out of the backyard of this house on the corner?"

"No. He was starting across the street when I first saw him."

"Then you do not know for a fact that he was coming out of the backyard. He could have been walking down the sidewalk from farther up Seventh Avenue, couldn't he?"

Officer Cooper shrugged and glanced at Sanchez. "He was crossing the street from the direction of the yard when I saw him."

"But," Eleanor Quake persisted, "you cannot say beyond a reasonable doubt that he came from that yard, can you?"

"No."

"You testified that you didn't actually see a fourth suspect leave the van or go through this gate." She placed her finger on the diagram. "You admitted you didn't actually see Francis Kelly leaving the backyard before crossing the street. And your highly trained dog, Primo, the best of all the dogs in the K-9 division, gave no indication that Francis Kelly was one of the suspects." She walked to the jury box. "Isn't it a fact, Sergeant Cooper," she said, looking from one juror's face to another, "that you had no basis whatever for assuming Francis Kelly had fled from the van you pursued?"

Cooper looked at Sanchez, who leaned slightly forward and stared back. "The suspect," Cooper said, "was wearing dark trousers, a gray sweatshirt, and a black baseball cap with the bill to the rear."

Twenty-One

"Circumstantial, Bear," said Kelly. "All circumstantial, that K-9 cop's testimony." They stood by the drinking fountain in the nearly empty corridor. The heat had driven most of the spectators out before Judge Blackwell stopped for the break. Everyone else fled to the cafeteria when she finally adjourned.

"The stuff he told about how dogs smell reminded me of the folklore we hear at Pow Wow," Sharmin said.

"He seemed pretty convincing to me," Bear said. "What if the jury believes him?"

"Don't you think Quack established reasonable doubt about my circumstance?" Kelly said.

"I do," said Sharmin.

Bear gazed down at Sharmin out of the corners of his eyes. "You can never tell what Asians are thinking, and you can't trust white people."

"You mean you don't even trust me, Bear?" Kelly said with a smile. "I'm a white man, remember."

"Um," Bear grunted, as if to say he had indeed forgotten. "But you must've been an Indian in a previous life. Most white people promise one thing and do the opposite. And black people," he looked at two African-American jurors who had returned from the cafeteria, "I don't like black people."

"You're a bit of a bigot, sometimes, blood brother," said Kelly, pulling a tissue from the pocket pack Soo Ling had insisted he take that morning. He had a scratchy throat and his nose was increasingly drippy. He blew into the tissue. "A hundred and nine degrees," he said, "and I've got a feeling I'm catching a summer cold. That's all I need."

Eleanor Quake clomped back from the direction of the elevators carrying a tall paper cup. Kelly walked over to her. "How do you think it looks so far?"

She thought a moment. "It's clear Sergeant Cooper chased the same van that fled from the robbery. If the jury believes everything he said about his dog Primo, they'll believe Wasser, X-Ray, and Bubba are the ones who jumped out of the van, and, therefore, must have committed the crime."

"I guess so," Kelly said thoughtfully. It was hard to accept, but maybe the other three were guilty. "But what about me, my circumstances?"

"Well," she drew on the straw sticking out of the paper cup, "I think my cross-examination sold reasonable doubt about you to every one of the jurors except the Japanese woman and the black man who wears glasses. "But," she said with a sigh, "if Sanchez keeps piling it on—" She began to tap her nose with her forefinger. "I keep wondering about the fourth culprit," she said. "Even though I tried to plant doubt about him during cross, there had to have been a fourth. The K-9 officer was probably right about the guy splitting from the other three and hiding in the yard next door. The crook was there when you crossed the street, maybe even watched you get arrested. When the cops had you, they stopped looking."

"Can't you tell the jury that?"

"If we had any evidence to support it, we could make it our case for the defense. Otherwise, the best we can do is suggest it during our closing argument." She turned her face to him. "By then, it could be too late."

Kelly walked back to where Bear and Sharmin were standing. Charlie Lawson, who greeted Kelly with a smile, had joined them.

"Lady Quake did a good job up there with that K-9 cop," he said.

"You think she sold the jury?" asked Kelly.

"I do." Lawson nodded emphatically. "She even convinced me." He grinned and punched Kelly playfully.

* * *

Shortly after the judge reconvened the trial, the air-conditioning came back on. Jury members applauded, Judge Blackwell smiled, and Bailiff Woznowski stood under the air vent and pretended to offer up a prayer of thanks. But Kelly felt chilled and shivered in his chair.

"How are you feeling?" asked Eleanor Quake.

"Not too terrific," he said nasally. He sounded like her now, he thought.

Prosecutor Sanchez called his next witness and spent ten minutes establishing that the female police officer who took the stand, along with another officer, was in the patrol car, which trapped Wasser, Bubba, and X-Ray at the office building. The witness gave her name as Margot Chung. A bit overweight, her uniform strained to contain her ample bosom and her badge rose and fell as she breathed like a bright leaf riding a wave. She identified the three defendants as the suspects she had arrested, then described how she and her partner handcuffed the suspects, read them their rights, and then searched them.

"What did you find when you searched the suspects?" Sanchez said.

"None of them was carrying a wallet or any identification, but suspect Wasser had a five-dollar bill in one pocket and some keys. Suspect Cox had a pair of leather gloves tucked in his belt, and a knife and forty-five cents in his pockets."

"Describe what the suspects were wearing."

"They all had on dark blue or black trousers, gray or white sweatshirts, and tennis sneakers."

Sanchez then brought out through questioning that Chung and her partner had transported the three suspects to the police station and booked them, after which she and her partner returned to the area where the arrests were made.

"At the time they were booked," Sanchez said, "was the height of each suspect noted?"

"Yes. Wade is six feet, two inches tall. Wasser is six three. Cox is six feet, five and a half."

Sanchez nodded. "You say you went back to the area where you made the arrest. What did you do when you went back?"

"We conducted a search of the yard the suspects ran through."

"Would you step out, please, and indicate on the diagram?"

"We searched this backyard here," she said as she pointed to the drawing. "And I found a pager in some tall grass by the fence between this yard and the house on the corner."

Sanchez went to his cartons, produced a pager, had it marked into evidence, and showed it to the witness. "Is this the pager you found?"

"Yes," she said. "It has my identification tag."

"What else did you find?"

"We didn't find anything else in the yard, but we conducted a search of the van in front of the house, and I found a Lakers' jacket, three black ski masks, two pairs of gloves, a cloth purse, a traveler's check made out to Circle K in the amount of twenty dollars, four rolls of coins—all quarters—a tire iron, a four-foot length of chain, and a box of Hershey bars."

Sanchez had her identify Camellia Brown's purse, then produced the other items she had named and had them marked. "I want to go back to the pager," he said. "Were you, at a later date, able to establish who the pager belonged to?"

"Yes. There is a sticker on the pager bearing the name 'Stay-In-Touch'. That's a local paging company. By checking the serial number on the pager, we were able to determine that Stay-In-Touch had registered that pager for service in the name of Francis Kelly."

As the jurors' eyes went to Kelly, he turned his head to Eleanor Quake. He had told her he had lost it and couldn't imagine how it turned up where it did. How was she going to handle this?

Carter Atwood was first to cross-examine. "Were the defendants, uh, given an opportunity to explain why they were at that office building?"

"Wade claimed they were on their way to see the building superintendent to try and sell their window-washing service," Chung replied.

"Thank you. No further questions."

Eleanor Quake began her cross-examination and was able to bring out that the Stay-In-Touch Company had no record of the pager being used after February 9th, the last time Kelly used it before he lost the pager.

"I had it when Soo Ling called me home from a skating party," he had told her. Soo Ling had fallen off a ladder. Amy had driven Kelly and Bear home in her uncle's car and they had rushed Soo Ling to the hospital.

"Isn't it possible," Eleanor Quake asked Chung, "that someone other than the defendant could have found the pager and used it through another paging company?"

"Anything's possible," replied Officer Chung, "but—"

"Thank you, no further questions."

"Redirect, Mr. Sanchez," Judge Blackwell said.

"Officer Chung," he said, rising and walking out from behind his table, "you testified that anything is possible—some unknown someone could have used the pager at a company other than Stay-In-Touch. Isn't it a fact that the defendant, Francis Kelly, could have used the pager with some other company? Isn't that possible?"

"Yes," Chung said, with a look of relief.

"And when you searched the van, did you find any kind of window-washing equipment, anything at all?"

"No, nothing."

Sanchez turned to go back to his table. "Oh," he said, stopping and looking at the jury, "did you ask the Stay-In-Touch company if Francis Kelly's pager had been reported lost or stolen?"

"Yes, we asked." Chung sat up confidently. "They had no record of it being reported lost or stolen."

Twenty-Two

In the men's restroom during the break, Kelly met the law student Charlie Lawson again.

"Is this a bum rap, or what?" Lawson said.

"It's a nightmare, man," replied Kelly. "It's worse than a nightmare. I'm almost starting to feel like I did last winter when I ran the marathon."

"Which marathon?" asked Lawson.

"That 26-miler that goes from Folsom all the way through town to the State Capitol."

"The California International Marathon?" exclaimed Lawson. "I didn't know you ran that. So did I. I run it every year."

"Really?" Kelly said. "Didn't see you, but there were so many—"He paused to blow his nose. "I only did it that one time. I've never trained for distance running, but a teacher asked me to do it for the Leukemia Society to raise funds, and I was in good shape from basketball so I figured I could handle it. But a really weird thing happened."

"What do you mean?"

"Well, I was just crossing the H Street bridge—I'd made it all that way, you know about three quarters of the distance—and I was really tired, of course, but all at once I felt like I was about ten feet under that ice water in the American River. I couldn't make my legs run anymore and I've never been so cold in my life. Everywhere I looked around me things were distorted and blurry."

"It sounds like you hit the wall," said Lawson.

"What?"

"They call it hitting the wall. It's what happens when your body runs out of fuel. Some call it 'bonking.'"

"I went bonkers, all right. It's the worst thing I ever went through. I could barely walk. It must've taken me a couple more hours to get to the finish line."

"Didn't you have any sports drink or energy bars with you?"

"I didn't even take any water along," Kelly replied with a sniffle.

"I'm surprised you made it as far as you did, and to continue on to the finish line after that without refueling your body is practically unheard of. You must've been in terrific shape."

"Well," murmured Kelly, "I couldn't let the Leukemia Society down."

Lawson nodded knowingly, then took a deep breath.. "I hit it just past Sac State."

"It happened to you, too?" Kelly said in surprise.

"It happens to almost every marathon runner. Your body can only store enough carbohydrates for about two hours of that kind of muscle demand. That's why you eat energy bars and sports drinks along the way. They put fuel into your system quickly. I had both with me or I wouldn't have been able to finish. Next year be sure to carry a supply with you."

Kelly shook his head vigorously. "I'm not running next year. There's no way I'm going through that again…at least I didn't think I'd ever feel that lousy again."

"If you're starting to feel that punk now, you'd better see a doctor," Lawson said.

"It's just this cold and this stupid trial getting me down. I was in the wrong place at the wrong time." Kelly blew his nose again. "Circumstances," he added with disgust.

"Well, hang in there. Your gal is plenty sharp."

"Everybody keeps telling me that."

As they stepped out of the restroom, Kelly said, "Hey, Leaper, why don't you come over to the house for some one-on-one when I get to feeling better? I'll clean your clock this time."

Lawson chuckled. "Think so? Maybe I will." He patted Kelly on the back. "Be sure to take care of that cold." He walked off with a friendly wave.

When Kelly returned to his place at the defendants' table, he found a small white envelope waiting on top of his yellow tablet. There was no name on it, no writing at all. The bailiff must've left it. He picked it up, and as he opened it, he sensed Wasser watching him, but when he glanced over, Wasser was staring at his pad of paper, doodling. The note read: "Can't come to court anymore. Uncle's mad at me for skipping work. – A."

Bummer, thought Kelly and put the note in his pocket as the short police patrolman, Daren "Buck" Rogers, took the stand.

This officer had one of those faces that would always look younger than its years, pink and boyish with a wide-eyed openness, and thick ears that reached out like catcher's mitts.

Rogers testified that he had been out of the academy a full eight months now, and this was his third appearance as a trial witness. He radiated self-confidence. When Sanchez had him describe the arrest of Kelly at the pay phone, Rogers told it as if, in all modesty, he had cracked the case almost single-handedly.

"Did you search the suspect after reading him his rights?" Sanchez asked.

"Yes, sir," Rogers said, deadly serious. "While maintaining control of the prisoner at all times, I performed a complete and thorough search of his person."

Sanchez looked at the ceiling and he almost smiled. "What did you find?"

"Two hundred and thirty-two dollars in United States currency, which I carefully placed in an evidence envelope and labeled with my name and badge number." The patrolman leaned back and glowed, obviously pleased with himself for a faultless performance.

"Your witness," Sanchez said, pulling at his nose to hide his smile.

For once, thought Kelly, Eleanor Quake was prepared. He'd seen this one coming and told her how his father sent the kitchen money for him and Soo Ling twice a month.

Eleanor Quake walked up to the witness. "Did the suspect tell you where he got the money?"

"Objection," Sanchez said. "That's—"

"I'll rephrase," Quake said quickly. "Did you ask the suspect where he got the money?"

Patrolman Rogers looked at the judge.

"You may answer," she said.

Satisfied that he was on safe ground, the patrolman turned to the jury and said with a smirk, "He said it was his allowance."

Laughs and titters came from the spectators.

Eleanor Quake waited until the snickering had quieted, then raised a hand holding a check-sized piece of paper. "If I were to tell you that I have a canceled check in the amount of 250 dollars made out to the defendant, signed by the defendant's father, and cashed the afternoon of March third by the defendant, that would explain where he got the money, wouldn't you say?"

"Objection, Your Honor." Sanchez rose to his feet. "The witness can't be asked to speculate about a piece of paper he hasn't even seen."

"Your Honor," said Eleanor Quake, "defense would place in evidence this check—"

"Objection!" Sanchez said, starting out from behind his table.

"Now," Judge Blackwell held up her hand to halt Sanchez, "this is not the proper time, Ms. Quake."

Eleanor Quake put her hand to her forehead. "Oh...sorry, Your Honor." She headed back to her seat. "No further questions."

Kelly almost grinned. Quack knew she was out of order, but the jury didn't know that she knew. They sure wouldn't forget how he got the money now.

Judge Blackwell said to the court clerk, "Strike everything after the witness saying, 'He said it was his allowance.'" She looked at the jury and said, "You will disregard that bit of business about the check."

Fat chance, thought Kelly. Not bad, Eleanor Quake. Not bad at all.

"Kathryn Miles," said the next witness. "I'm chief identification technician for the Sacramento Police Department." She was a prim woman in her late forties with graying red hair. She had a small, dark mole next to the corner of her mouth, as if to punctuate each declarative sentence that came from her pale, thin lips. Kathryn Miles, period. Chief identification technician, period.

Sanchez began to draw out the woman's experience and credentials until defense stipulated that she was an expert.

She told of examining the van and all of the articles in evidence for fingerprints. Then she described in detail how prints were removed from the items, including one of Kelly's prints from the cash he was carrying when arrested.

"The people will enter into evidence these photo enlargements of the finger prints," Sanchez said, producing photos that were tagged and shown to the jury.

"Print number two," said the witness, "was taken from the candy box, prints three and four from the pager, number five from the wallet, and six, seven, and eight from the van. Print number three from the pager was a near match to defendant Kelly's. Due to the imperfect condition of the print, we were unable to classify it a 100-percent match."

"Were you able to determine a positive identification for prints two, four, or five?" asked Carter Atwood on cross-examination.

"No."

"Did any of the prints found in the van match the defendants'?"

"No."

Eleanor Quake asked, "You testified, did you, that you compared all of the fingerprints to those taken from the defendants when they were booked at the police station?"

"Yes."

"Were comparison tests also made to prints on file with the Department of Motor Vehicles, or the FBI, or any other government branch?"

"No. Our instructions specified only the suspects."

"Thank you. No more questions, Your Honor."

As she sat back down, Eleanor Quake whispered to Kelly, "We may have discovered a pinhole in the D.A.'s case."

While Judge Blackwell and Sanchez held a conference at the bench, Kelly whispered to Eleanor Quake, "I've got an idea. The fourth robber, the one who got away, he could be some pal of the guy who got shot."

"I thought of that, too," said Eleanor Quake. "If they had checked the fingerprints with DMV or the FBI, they might have found out who it was. It's certainly a reasonable possibility." She looked at Kelly and tapped her nose thoughtfully.

"What?" Kelly said.

"Just thinking," she replied. "Tell me about your friend, that big, black-haired boy you always talk to in the hall."

"You mean Bear?"

"Is that what everybody calls him?"

"That's his name, William Tall Bear. He's a full-blooded Kummeyaay Indian. His dad runs the casino on their reservation east of San Diego. Bear's the best friend I've got. Why do you want to know about him?"

Eleanor Quake looked steadily into Kelly's eyes. "You're not going to like this, but..." She shifted her gaze to her legal pad on the table. "Remember Shakespeare's story about Julius Caesar and his good friend Brutus?"

"'Et tu, Brute,'" Kelly quoted. "What's that got to do—"

"It's not unusual to be done in by someone close to you," said Eleanor Quake, locking eyes with him again. "Do you know where William Tall Bear was at the time you were arrested?"

"That's ridiculous," he said angrily, frowning. Bear's remark about not liking black people flashed in his mind, but he shoved it aside. "Ridiculous," he repeated.

Twenty-Three

As the court clerk swore in Jamal Spoon, Kelly looked at the tall African-American boy and wondered where he fit into all this. Jamal had the threatening demeanor of a Masai warrior and he was dressed entirely in black: black, long-sleeved shirt with black buttons, black slacks, black belt, and black loafers without socks, so the black skin of his ankles was exposed. Ramrod straight and square shouldered, his gleaming eyes never blinked as he took the oath. He hadn't spoken to Kelly since that bus ride when they were in the YMCA basketball program in sixth grade. Kelly wondered if Jamal had been in that Circle-K when it was robbed.

After Sanchez got Jamal to tell his name and that he was a student at Martin Luther King High School, he asked, "Did you attend Roosevelt High School most of your freshman year?"

"Yes."

"And did you try out for the freshman basketball team while you were a student at Roosevelt High?"

"Yes."

"Did you make the team?"

"Yes. I was on the starting five."

"In your own words," said Sanchez, "tell us what happened during that year that involved one of the defendants in this case."

"Bubba Cox told me I'd never play varsity ball and roughed me up."

"You are referring to Bernard Cox, seated at the defendant's table?"

"That's right," said Jamal, glaring at Bubba.

"What do you mean, he roughed you up?"

"He knocked me down with his fist."

"What did you do?"

"I told him, 'You don't decide who plays, you ain't Coach Hinman.' And he said, 'No, I ain't the coach. I'm the coach's messenger.'"

Sanchez looked at the jury. "He said, 'I'm coach Hinman's messenger'?"

"That's right," Jamal replied. "Then he kicked me two, three times and broke my ribs."

"And that's the reason you left—"

"Objection, Your Honor," said Wilson Wilson. "He's leading the witness."

"I'll rephrase," Sanchez said. "What did you do after that?"

"I transferred to Martin Luther King."

"Do you play on the basketball team there?"

"Yessir. I'm on the starting five since tenth grade."

"And were you named to the all-city team of the Sacramento Metro League last season?"

"Yessir, and the year before."

Sanchez walked to the evidence table and began to dig through one of the cartons. "I want to ask you about the incident that occurred during the game between Martin Luther King and Roosevelt High at the city tournament last season."

Eleanor Quake looked at Kelly questioningly. He shook his head.

Sanchez took a newspaper page from the cardboard carton. "I have here," he said, "the sports page from the *Sacramento Bee*, dated January twenty-second." He displayed the paper to the defense attorneys, then carried it to Jamal. "Have you read this story headlined 'Riot Mars Playoff Game?'"

"Yes," replied Jamal.

"Does it fairly state what happened during that game?"

"Pretty much."

Sanchez handed the paper to the court clerk. "This will be people's exhibit number 23." He moved back to Jamal. "Tell us in your own words what—" Sanchez stopped. "First, did you play in that game?"

"Yes," said Jamal, nodding, "until I got hurt in the third period."

"How did you get hurt?"

"Bubba Cox elbowed me up 'longside my face and broke my jaw."

"Then what happened?"

"My team went after Cox, and players came off the bench and a lot of the fans got into it."

"It caused a riot, did it not?" Sanchez said. "Bernard Cox's unprovoked attack on you caused—"

"I object, Your Honor," said Wilson W. Wilson. "The defendants are not charged with fighting at a ball game. All of this has nothing to do with the crime in this case."

"It goes to motive, Your Honor," said Sanchez.

"Objection overruled," the judge said.

"Now," Sanchez said, walking back to his table and glancing at his notes, "I want to ask you next if any of the other defendants ever did anything that, in your opinion, showed that they hated African-Americans."

"Objection, Your Honor," said Carter Atwood, tugging at his tie. "Calls for a conclusion by—"

"I'll allow it," said Judge Blackwell.

"Any of them do anything?" Sanchez repeated to Jamal.

"All of them," said Jamal, causing Kelly to look up sharply. Eleanor Quake eyed him again.

"Can you be more specific?" Sanchez said.

"One time, Kelly—"

"You're talking about the defendant, Francis Kelly?" Sanchez said.

Eleanor Quake whispered, "What?" at Kelly, but he stared mystified at Jamal.

"Yeah," continued the witness. "One time I was on a bus with him, riding home from the Y downtown, and he stood up all the way because the only empty seat was next to a black man."

"Francis Kelly refused to sit next to an African-American?" Sanchez said.

"Correct," said Jamal.

Kelly quickly scrawled a note to Eleanor Quake. "That's not the whole story," he wrote.

"At this time," Judge Blackwell announced, "we will take our break. We will continue with this witness when we reconvene."

Twenty-Four

Isolated at a corner table in the cafeteria, Eleanor Quake stirred the ice in her cold drink with a straw and waited for Kelly to explain.

"That happened way back in sixth grade," he said. "When we got on the bus, there were only two seats open. Jamal was ahead of me, and he passed up the one next to the old black man and took the other seat. When I got there, I could see why. The old man was sprawled across the seat, mumbling to himself. The front of his shirt was all stained and you could smell liquor and vomit from him. I just stood there a minute and the old man stared at me, his eyes bloodshot and watery, and all at once he reached out and grabbed my wrist. He rubbed his hand on mine and said, 'It don't come off, see? The color don't come off.' I jerked my hand free and moved on back in the bus where Jamal was sitting. I did stand up until we got off the bus."

Eleanor Quake said nothing.

"Then Jamal said to me, 'I'll never forgive you for doing that.' I go, 'What did I do?' And he goes, 'Don't play dumb. You wouldn't sit with that old man just because he was black.' I thought Jamal was joking, and I go, 'Because he was black? You've got to be kidding. Why didn't you sit with him?' He goes, 'Well, he was drunk and he smelled, but it's different for me.'"

Kelly waited, but Eleanor Quake still said nothing so he continued, "I said. 'Why? Because you're black? I can't find someone offensive for the same reasons you do just because I'm white, is that what you're saying?' Jamal never even answered. Just stomped off and never spoke to me again. That old man might have been a fine person any other time, but that day he had puke on his shirt and smelled sour as owl manure. His color didn't matter. I wouldn't have sat with him if he'd been fourteen karat gold."

Eleanor Quake peered at him, turning the drink cup in her fingers. "I believe you," she said. "But there's no way I can make it clear on cross-examination. We'll have to bring it out when we present our defense."

"But everything is still circumstantial," Kelly said. "Why should we present a defense?"

"Juries have convicted on circumstantial evidence many times," said Eleanor Quake. "Barring a miracle, like our missing bandit turning himself in and confessing, it's looking more and more like we may have to present a defense."

She delicately wiped her mouth with a paper napkin, then tucked the napkin into the empty cup. "If we do present a defense," she said, looking at the ceiling, "the only thing we have to counter the inferences the prosecution has drawn for the jury is to put you on the stand and let you tell your side of the story. Sanchez will tear into you on cross-examination. It's a big risk. He's very good." She looked at him. "I have to know how you really feel, deep inside, about racism."

She waited, but Kelly didn't know how to respond.

At length, she said, "Surely you have an opinion one way or the other."

"Well—" He blew his nose and groped for words. "There's no way you're going to like every person in the world, but you can't hate everyone who is different than you are. You try to understand them, or just accept them and respect their differences. Hate is self-destructive. It uses you up."

"Hate does?"

Kelly sneezed.

"Bless you," said Eleanor Quake. "So, you think racial hate is self-destructive."

"Big time," he said with a nod, and blew his nose. "Besides, it's stupid. You know, ignorance. People who do this kind of thing because someone's not like them are stupid. Or maybe afraid."

"Afraid?"

"Yeah. Lots of times people feel threatened by things they don't understand, even if they won't admit it. They might not even realize that's what it is."

"So, what's the answer to racial conflict?"

"People just have to get to know those who are different."

"Like you know your Indian friends, and your Chinese housekeeper, and black boys you shoot baskets with?"

"Right. When you get to know them, you don't feel threatened."

"That's rather simplistic, isn't it?"

"Maybe so," Kelly said with a shrug. "It works for me. People just have to get to know more."

"Who's going to make them learn?"

Kelly turned and looked out the window. "I don't know. It's not up to me."

"Isn't it? Did you ever speak out about this to X-Ray, Bubba, or Wasser?"

Kelly shook his head.

"To anybody?"

"No."

"Too bad," Eleanor Quake said.

They sat in silence for a few minutes, Eleanor Quake staring at her empty cup, Kelly pondering what she had said.

"What's your book about?" he asked suddenly.

Eleanor Quake's eyes widened, as if taken by surprise.

"Carol told me you hadn't been trying any cases for a while, until this one came along, because you were living in Berkeley writing a book. What's it about?"

"Well," she said as she looked deeply into his eyes, "it's about people like you, Kelly."

"Like me?"

"That's right. People who think racial bigotry and society's other ills are wrong and need to be fixed, but not by them. Somebody else should do it. I haven't settled on a title yet. Right now, I have it labeled 'If You're Not Part of the Solution, You're Part of the Problem.'"

"Ironic," Kelly said. "That's another of Coach Hinman's favorite sayings."

"I know." She nodded. "It's trite, but it does make the point."

It was time to get back to the courtroom, and she pushed back her chair and stood up. "Have you heard the old joke about the guy crossing the street who got hit by a bus?"

Kelly shook his head.

"The bus driver jumped out and ran back to help him. The guy was badly hurt–all battered and bleeding–but he was dragging himself down the gutter away from the scene of the accident. 'What are you doing?' says the bus driver. The guy says, 'I don't want to get involved.'"

Kelly laughed, but Eleanor Quake stared at him seriously.

"Hasn't this trial made you want to try to make a difference? Do you have to get hit by a bus?"

Twenty-Five

Another envelope was waiting at his place at the defendants' table when Kelly returned. He opened it and removed and unfolded an 8 by 10 piece of paper. It was a flyer announcing a rally of "Native Americans and friends" at the state capitol. The rally Sharmin had asked him about, he remembered. There was no note or signature on the handbill or the envelope. He glanced back in the courtroom where Bear and Sharmin were sitting. Sharmin appeared to be reading something, but Bear saw him looking at them and nodded with a slight smile.

One of them must've left the envelope, Kelly thought, shaking his head. He refolded the flyer, stuck it back in the envelope, and shoved it into a pocket. As he did this, he recognized another face among the spectators. It was IQ Reid, the thin black boy who had taken to living on the streets. IQ bobbed his head and waved with a big smile when he saw Kelly looking at him. What's that two-faced liar doing here? thought Kelly.

He put another tissue to his nose and blew gently as Judge Blackwell called for the proceedings to begin. When Eleanor Quake and the other defense attorneys declined to cross-examine Jamal Spoon, basketball coach Nels Hinman was called to the witness stand.

Thick-lipped, glowering, blond hair askew, Hinman walked past the jurors as if they weren't there, his arrogant attitude proclaiming disdain and disgust–a lion trapped in an inferior's snare.

Prosecutor Sanchez asked the judge for permission to treat Hinman as a hostile witness. He then spent ten minutes asking questions to establish that the coach knew each of the defendants and had worked with them for several years molding them into a close-knit team. Then Sanchez fooled with papers on his table for several minutes.

He's getting ready, Kelly thought. We're finally going to learn why the coach was called to testify.

"How long have you been coaching?" Sanchez asked.

"Fifteen years."

"On any team you have coached, have there ever been any African-American players?"

"No." Coach shook his head. "I've never coached any blacks."

"Have there ever been any Asian Americans?"

"No."

"Any Hispanics?"

"No." The coach leaned back and crossed his legs, eyeing Sanchez like he was watching a snake.

"Would you say that part of your job is to help form the character of the young men you coach?"

"I would say that's a big part of a coach's job, yes."

"So, you feel a responsibility to pass on to them–to teach them–your values?"

The coach nodded solemnly. "Lord knows, somebody's got to."

"What exactly is it," said Sanchez, stepping closer and facing the coach squarely, "that you are trying to teach them by refusing to have any non-white players on your team?"

Coach Hinman's eyes narrowed to the squinty slits Kelly had seen so often. "The foreign boys never try out for varsity basketball at Roosevelt," he said evenly. "I don't know why."

Sanchez turned and stared at Bubba. He appeared to be about to say something, but changed his mind. He walked over, consulted his notes, then looked back at the coach. "Did you not, during the City Tournament, direct Bernard Cox to put Jamal Spoon, an African-American, out of the game?"

"That question is an insult," Hinman growled, looking at Judge Blackwell.

"Answer the question," said the judge.

"I may have told Bubba to guard him close," said Hinman. "Yes, that was it. Guard him real close, I said."

"Did you penalize him in any way for inflicting the injury on Jamal Spoon?" Sanchez said.

"Penalize him?" The coach looked at Sanchez curiously. "What for?"

"It caused a riot, didn't it?"

Coach merely shrugged.

"And then you lost that game, which put you out of the tournament, isn't that correct?"

Coach Hinman looked at the floor. "That was because of the lousy officiating," he snarled.

"But you took no corrective action against Bernard Cox, did you, because he had been following your orders to get Jamal Spoon."

"Objection, Your Honor," said Wilson Wilson.

"Sustained," said Judge Blackwell. "You can't answer your own question, Mr. Sanchez."

"I'll withdraw it, Your Honor," said Sanchez. "I have no further questions of this witness."

"The jury will disregard that last question," Judge Blackwell said. "Defense may cross-examine."

The attorneys looked at each other. Carter, Kite, and Wilson Wilson shook their heads. Kite said, "We have no questions for this witness, Your Honor."

Eleanor Quake spoke up. "I have, Your Honor." She looked at Hinman, but remained in her chair. "Have you ever seen Francis Kelly with any of the other defendants when they were not playing basketball?"

Hinman scratched his jaw, looking at Kelly. "Can't say I have."

"So, to the best of your knowledge, they were associated only as members of the basketball team. Is that a fair statement?"

"I guess so," he replied.

"Let the record show the witness answered yes," Eleanor Quake said to the judge.

"Agreed." Judge Blackwell motioned to the court recorder.

"I have no further questions."

"The witness is excused," the judge said, throwing the coach a look that, Kelly thought, conveyed a mental karate chop. Or possibly something more lethal.

Coach Hinman slowed as he walked out past the defendants' table. He flashed a thumbs-up sign to X-Ray. Kelly saw it and lowered his aching head to rest on his hands. Hinman's testimony had been unsettling. The idea of playing another season under the blatant bigot's direction troubled him. But if he refused to play–like a protest–would it make any difference? He decided to give it more thought when he felt better and all this was over.

Judge Blackwell declared a recess and Kelly left the courtroom to rap with Bear. IQ Reid appeared to be waiting for him in the corridor, but stood well away from Bear and Sharmin.

Kelly glared over at IQ. "Give me a couple of minutes, Bear. I'm going to tell IQ what a jerk he is."

Bear and Sharmin headed off toward the windows at the end of the corridor and Kelly strode up to IQ. "You lied to me, IQ. You used the money I gave you to buy booze. I saw you on the riverbank."

"It wasn't a lie when I said it, Kelly," IQ said earnestly. "It was those two babes. They sweet-talked me into it. But," he added quickly, "I've dumped them. They were a bad influence. Temptation and Infatuation, I called 'em. But I said to myself, you gotta put temptation and infatuation behind you, man, and get on with your life."

He rubbed his hands together as if washing off the girls' and their wicked influence. "I did go make it up with Uncle Fred, my cousin's stepfather. I'm back living there now, and getting straight."

Kelly looked steadily at the smaller boy, not sure whether to believe him. "So, what are you doing downtown, then?"

"It's part of my new plan, see. I'm going back to school when it starts and get into the writing business. But, I figure on getting a jumpstart on it. Today, I'm going to see a guy at the *Sacramento Bee* about doing a special series on teens that live on the streets. I'll write about things I've seen and stories I've heard from those dumpster-divers who live out there. I mean, I've heard cases of child abuse that rip your heart out…like, there's a homeless Asian girl they call China Doll. She's got tattoos of dragons all over her body. She says her father sold her to a 50-year old man in New York when she was eleven—a 50-year old man! So she ran away. Came clear across the country in a hearse with a corpse that was being brought out here for burial. Spooky, man. And this homeless guy 'Wheels,' he came to Sacramento from Seattle on his skateboard. Before that, he'd lived with his stepfather in Europe for two years. The old man threw him out one day after an argument. Wheels went all over Europe on his skateboard—to Germany, Austria, and Italy. He did Berlin, Rome, Venice." IQ chuckled. "I guess he couldn't skateboard in Venice. But, I tell ya, man, there's a zillion stories begging to be told."

IQ was so earnestly enthusiastic, Kelly caught his spirit. "That's terrific, IQ. You'll make a great writer."

A bailiff walked past them and the sight snapped Kelly back to reality. "What are you doing here at the trial?"

IQ's face blanked momentarily, but he quickly resumed his enthusiastic attitude. "There could be an angle for another story here. You know: 'Teens On Trial.' I could write it from your viewpoint, the way you and the other jocks see it. Nobody's doing that." He paused for a few seconds. "And, uh, another thing is...before I meet with the guy at the newspaper, I figure I ought to change my looks." He waved a hand to his clothes. He was wearing a pair of reasonably clean shorts and a T-shirt with an advertiser's slogan printed on it. "For just a few bucks I can buy a white shirt and some slacks at the thrift store—maybe even a tie. I couldn't ask ol' Uncle Fred for any cash, he doesn't trust me that much, yet. So—" His eyes flashed down the hall to where Bear and Sharmin were standing, then back to Kelly. "Could you stake me?"

Kelly's hand reached to his pocket as he, too, glanced down the hall at Bear. "I could lend you five bucks, I guess."

IQ took the money. "Thanks, man." He turned quickly and headed for the elevators.

Knowing that Bear would disapprove of what he had done, Kelly decided to not talk about it no matter what Bear said. He strolled down the hall and joined the two Indians at the window.

"Take a look," said Bear, gesturing to the street below.

Kelly looked. On the other side of the street from the courthouse were the two blond girls who had been with IQ that day in the tunnel. Temptation and Infatuation, he called them. As Kelly watched, the girls waved to someone approaching them from the courthouse immediately below him. In a second, IQ came into view. He crossed the street and joined the girls, saying something, apparently, because one of them clapped him on the back and the other kissed his cheek. Then the three of them walked to the corner and left Kelly's view.

"Damn," muttered Kelly. "Fool me once, shame on you. Fool me twice, shame on me. I swallowed IQ's con like a stupid tourist buys the Golden Gate Bridge." He glanced at Bear, then hung his head and blew his nose.

"Deceit," said Bear, "is not good."

Kelly nodded in sad agreement. "That's what I get for meddling in other people's lives."

Twenty-Six

"The people call John Pernell," said District Attorney Sanchez.

A middle-aged man neatly dressed in a business suit took the stand and was sworn in. He reminded Kelly of a Hong Kong Brit–well tailored, educated, gray at the temples, a professional man. Sanchez walked to him and said, "Would you state your name and occupation, please."

"John Pernell. I'm a field agent for the Federal Bureau of Investigation."

Kelly blew his nose. FBI? What in the world?

"For the past three years," agent Pernell continued, "I have been assigned to a special division monitoring organizations believed to be antigovernment or antisocial and radical in nature."

The prosecutor walked to the evidence table and picked out the photograph of the van. He handed it to the witness. "In this picture of the vehicle used in the robbery," Sanchez said, "there is a sticker in the rear window bearing the letters R-A-H-O-W-A. Do those letters have any special significance?"

"Yes," replied the witness. "They stand for Racial Holy War, a slogan or rallying cry of some of the organizations we monitor."

Sanchez returned to his cartons and produced another photograph, which was marked into evidence. "I show you this photograph taken March eighteenth of this year at the county jail by a police department photographer. Can you identify the young man pictured without his shirt on?"

Agent Pernell glanced at the photo. "It's the defendant, Ray Wade."

"I call your attention to the tattoo on his chest, approximately over his heart. Would you describe it to the jury and explain its significance, please?"

"He has the number eighty-eight tattooed there," said Pernell. "To members of white-supremacist groups, eighty-eight stands for heil Hitler."

Kelly's stomach knotted. He remembered seeing X-Ray's tattoo, but had never asked what it meant. He swallowed gingerly. His throat was so sore, the back of his head and neck ached.

"Are any of the defendants known to be involved with white-supremacist groups?" Sanchez said.

"Bernard Cox and Jeffrey Wasser were picked up last summer in Oakland. They were with a group of Fourth Reich Skinheads that marched and burned a cross in a city park. They were released and no charges were filed."

Kelly sat stunned. How could he have been blind to all this?

Eleanor Quake scribbled on her yellow pad and slid it over to him. She had written: "Circumstantial??"

Prosecutor Sanchez walked up close to the judge and they exchanged words in hushed voices.

"Counsel approach," Judge Blackwell said.

The defense attorneys went to the bench and another sidebar discussion took place. In a few moments, the defense attorneys went back to their seats, and Judge Blackwell turned to the jurors.

"Members of the jury," she said, "a man named Jake Russell is also under indictment for this crime. He was shot during the commission of the robbery and is in critical condition in the hospital, therefore not present in court. You are going to hear testimony about Jake Russell, as it has a bearing on the defendants." She looked at the district attorney. "Mr. Sanchez."

"Agent Pernell," Sanchez said, "are you acquainted with one Jake Russell?"

"Yes, I am."

"Would you please tell the jury how you came by this acquaintance?"

"Jake Russell," stated the witness, looking directly at the jurors, "is a known member of a white supremacist organization called the Aryan Brotherhood, which he joined when he was incarcerated at Folsom Prison. The Bureau keeps tabs on such individuals, and I was on a surveillance team which observed him for a period last year."

"Your Honor," Sanchez said, "The people enter into evidence this photo enlargement at this time." He withdrew another 12 by 14 picture from one of the cartons.

"It will be exhibit number 24," said the judge.

The clerk put the photograph in a plastic envelope and affixed a sticker to the envelope. Then Sanchez carried it to the witness. "Do you recognize this picture?"

"Yes. It's a picture I took with a telephoto lens at a rock concert August tenth of last year. It shows Jake Russell and Richard Sims, another member of the Aryan Brotherhood, who were in the audience at the concert. And with them—sort of between them in the photo—is one of the defendants in this case."

"Can you positively identify that defendant from this picture?" Sanchez took the picture and displayed it to the members of the jury.

"Yes," said the FBI man. "It's the one near the end of the table, Francis Kelly."

Judge Blackwell adjourned for the day, after asking Agent Pernell to return for cross-examination. The court began to clear and Kelly's eyes fell on Charlie Lawson who had stopped at the door and was looking back at him. No longer leapin' Lawson, acquaintance, fellow sports enthusiast, and sympathizer, the man's glare said "guilty" so loudly it echoed in Kelly's head.

"I wasn't with those two guys at the concert," he said to Eleanor Quake, feeling the sweat run down his back. "I went with Bear. We must've been sitting behind them, and the picture makes it look like we were together."

"It does," Eleanor Quake agreed, rubbing her eyes wearily. "Do you see now what circumstantial evidence can mean, how convincing it can be?"

"Convincing," he said numbly, as the image of Charlie Lawson's cold stare burned in his mind's eye. What if the people on the jury were like Lawson? He wiped his nose with a tissue and moaned. "Circumstantial. Oh, yes." He pushed back his chair. "I've got to get out of here." The paneled walls of the courtroom seemed to be closing in on him, like a noose tightening. His raw throat cried out for relief, and his head was pounding. He was hitting another wall.

Twenty-Seven

The steady V-8 roar and softness of the custom upholstery coaxed Kelly's eyes closed. He slumped between Bear, who drove, and Sharmin, who hummed softly.

"Where are we going?" murmured Kelly, shivering in spite of the heat.

"You'll find out," Bear said.

"We should tell him," Sharmin said to Bear. "Francis, we're going up to the Miwok reservation near Clear Lake. You're going to be our guest at the steam ceremony."

"Really?" he said, struggling to stay awake. "I've wanted to do that sometime. But I have to be in court tomorrow morning." His eyelids slowly dropped shut.

"We'll get you there," Sharmin said, stroking his hair. She began to hum again.

It was dark when they woke him. "I must've slept for hours," he said.

"You did," Sharmin said. "Come on." She took his hand. "This way."

They followed Bear up a slope to a cluster of men, women, and children gathered around a large fire filled with rocks the size of cantaloupes.

Bear and Sharmin left Kelly and walked over to one of the older men. Each of them placed something in the man's hand.

"What did you give him?" Kelly said when they returned.

"Tobacco," said Bear.

"It represents our wishes," Sharmin said, "to be passed on to the Creator. We gave him some for you, too."

"I wish—" Kelly began, but his fevered brain couldn't sort out what he wished the most. "Can't think straight," he mumbled.

"Never mind," said Sharmin. "When we go in the lodge, just think of this: the sweat is Mother Earth's womb. Thank her for her womb, and focus your mind on something – anything but yourself."

"Strip down to your shorts," said Bear, who was removing his own clothes.

Kelly struggled out of his shirt. The chill mountain air caused him to shudder and sneeze.

"It gets hot in there," Bear said, smearing himself with the sacred smoke as the others were doing. "You can't see, can't move, can't hardly breathe. You'll suffer some."

"You're supposed to," Sharmin said as she smeared smoke on Kelly's arms and face, her touch soft and tender.

One of the men placed a shovel in the fire and scooped out a load of the big stones. They were now so hot, they seemed translucent. The man carried them into the low, round lodge nearby, then returned for more.

"When we get inside," said Sharmin, "rub this on your skin." She gave Kelly a branch of sage leaves.

"Come on," Bear said. "It's time."

One by one, the participants dropped to their knees and crawled into the steamy blackness of the lodge, forming a human coil inside. At first, they sat, squeezed together in silence. Kelly welcomed the warmth after the chill he had experienced outside. As the heat grew in intensity, a man's voice offered up a prayer to the Grandfather Spirits. Then the gathering began to sing. At length, the group fell into silent prayer and the steam steadily thickened.

Kelly coughed frequently and trembled. When he inhaled, the air scalded the membranes in his nose. The heat pressed down like a thousand unrelenting suns, and he wanted to throw up. Just then, the flap door of the lodge opened, letting in a gust of delicious oxygen. A hand reached in and delivered a long Indian pipe. The flap closed again and the pipe was passed around, each man, woman, and child first tapping it on the ground, then taking a puff.

Kelly's head spun dizzily, his mind flashing weird lights and colors. Was it his illness, he wondered, or the ancient ceremony? He remembered Bear telling him it symbolized the cycle of creation, death, and rebirth. His life was in a shambles, but it didn't seem to matter at this moment.

"Thank you, Mother Earth," he murmured, and he felt Sharmin's hot, moist hand press his arm.

Twenty-Eight

"You look better today," Eleanor Quake said as she approached Kelly, who was waiting with Bear and Sharmin outside the courtroom.

"Feelin' better, almost like a new man," he said with a sniffle.

"I'm glad to hear that," Eleanor Quake said in her nasal monotone.

"I've got a feeling," Kelly said. "Something important is going to happen today. Something that will give this case a whole, different look."

"Is that so," Eleanor quake said without enthusiasm.

The courtroom door swung abruptly open and Bailiff Woznowski urged the waiting crowd inside.

When everyone had taken seats, the Bailiff intoned, "All rise," and Judge Blackwell made her entrance.

FBI agent Pernell was recalled to the stand and the defense attorneys began their cross-examination. Kelly listened intently, but the questioning seemed hollow and unproductive. Where's the big break? he kept thinking.

In the middle of one of agent Pernell's responses, a court clerk silently came out of the door behind Judge Blackwell. The clerk slipped up behind the judge and handed her a piece of paper. Judge Blackwell read the note, then interrupted Pernell with a slam of her gavel. "Court will stand in recess," she declared. "I want to see counsel in my chambers immediately."

The attorneys rose and quickly followed the judge through the door behind the bench. Kelly smiled inwardly. This could be it—the big break.

The bailiff did not escort the jury out. He had received no instructions from the judge, so he sat at his table and looked at his hands. The deputies, also lacking direction from the judge, decided not to take X-ray and Bubba out, so Kelly kept his seat. As the minutes crawled by, a few spectators got up and went out to the hall. The others spoke in hushed tones. Kelly began to imagine what was happening in the judge's chambers.

"I just received word," Judge Blackwell might be saying, "that four young men have been arrested at a Circle K store in East Sacramento where they had just robbed and beaten everyone. They were driving a white van. It looks like they are the ones who should be on trial here not Kelly, Wade, Cox, and Wasser."

Kelly shook his head. Even if that happened, the D.A. wouldn't back off this case. He has too much evidence. He's laid it all out for the jury and they believe him. They believe we're all guilty.

But what if...Judge Blackwell says, "A prisoner at the jail has told one of the jailers that X-Ray Wade told him all about the robbery and Kelly wasn't involved. This prisoner will testify in exchange for a reduction of his own sentence."

That idea appealed to Kelly, but as he continued to turn it over in his mind, he decided it was an extremely long shot. X-Ray wasn't much of a talker and his lawyer had specifically told him not to talk to anybody. Bubba probably got the same instructions from Wilson Wilson Wilson. Kelly put that idea aside and fancied another possibility.

What if...a Roosevelt High student Kelly hardly knew happened to live on 7th Avenue? This kid's been on vacation until today. This morning he read in the paper about the trial and immediately telephoned the court because he remembered looking out his window back on March third and seeing Kelly walking past his house on 7th Avenue at exactly 4:45 in the afternoon. Kelly couldn't have been in the van or in that back yard. He's innocent!

This was a great idea—a perfect alibi.

But why hadn't the kid come forward before now?

Because he doesn't exist, Kelly told himself reluctantly. None of these daydreams was good enough. It will have to be something really solid. Like…a guy is arrested in a stolen car crossing the state line into Nevada. He has rolls of coins and one of those traveler's checks made out to Circle K. The cops grill him and he confesses. He is the fourth robber. Kelly is innocent!

This was the best idea. Kelly stared at the door to the judge's chambers hopefully. Ten minutes became fifteen, then twenty. It's something big, all right, he thought. My guardian angel has come through.

Finally the door to the judge's chambers swung open and Judge Blackwell appeared followed by the defense attorneys. Eleanor Quake's brow was furrowed and she avoided Kelly's eyes as she took her seat.

"What?" Kelly said.

"You'll find out now," she whispered.

Judge Blackwell gaveled for silence and immediately addressed the jury. "The man, Jake Russell, who was also indicted for the crimes being tried in this case, died less than an hour ago from the wound he received during the robbery."

She turned from the jury. "Mr. Sanchez."

He rose. "Your Honor, the people now enter a motion, under Section 189 of the California Penal Code. We move to add the charge of murder to those pending in the case before this court."

"So ordered," Judge Blackwell said over the gasps and murmurs of the spectators.

Kelly could not believe what he had heard.

Judge Blackwell rapped her gavel and turned again to the jury. "When you begin deliberations, I will explain to you and give you written copies of the law pertaining to each of the charges in this case–including this latest. But let me tell you now that, under the Felony Murder Rule in California law, if a suspect is killed during the commission of the crime, his accomplice or accomplices may be held accountable."

"This is bull!" said Bubba loudly.

"No," said the judge. "This is justice, Mr. Cox."

The fresh and optimistic outlook Kelly had enjoyed since his rebirth at the steam ceremony had been destroyed in minutes. When all four defense attorneys begged for a recess to discuss the new development with their clients, Judge Blackwell adjourned the court. They were to reconvene at 10:00 the next morning.

Twenty-Nine

Eleanor Quake and Kelly lingered outside the courtroom like mourners at a funeral. Bear and Sharmin had left after a few words with Kelly. Only two or three people were scattered down the third floor corridor. "What are we going to do?" Kelly said with a groan, rubbing his forehead with his palms.

Eleanor Quake shook her head for what seemed like minutes, then finally murmured nasally, "If we could only find the fourth robber." She took a deep breath and sighed. "I asked that FBI agent, Pernell, if he would run the fingerprints that are in evidence through the government's computer files. He wasn't encouraging. Said a request would have to be submitted through the proper channels. It would have to go to Washington for approval, etcetera, etcetera."

It was a ray of hope, a faint and tenuous ray, but Kelly grasped it. "The fingerprints, right."

Eleanor Quake pulled at her lip, deep in thought and Kelly watched her silently until footsteps approaching from the elevators drew his attention.

It was his father.

Handsome as always, he came in giant, purposeful strides. He was not dressed for Sacramento. With a gray fedora in one hand, a black mohair overcoat over his arm, and his three-piece charcoal gray suit, he looked like he could've just left the U.S. Embassy in Moscow. Perhaps he had.

"It's not over, is it?" his father said, joining them.

"No," said Kelly. "What are you doing here? I thought—"

"I talked to Charlie Lawson late yesterday," his father said. "Flew all night. I knew Charlie had to be wrong." His eyes searched Kelly's.

"He is, Dad. I'm innocent. And things have suddenly gotten worse. Now I'm charged with murder!"

His father's face looked stunned, then his eyes snapped to Eleanor Quake, who explained the latest developments.

As he digested her explanation, the elder Kelly put his arm around his son. For the first time since the opening day of the trial, Kelly felt his father's full support. At times like this, he admitted to himself, his chosen role as a loner seemed blindly egotistic.

"What needs to be done?" his father said to Eleanor Quake.

She shook her head with a worried look.

"The fingerprints," Kelly said. "They could be from the guy that was with Jake Russell at the rock concert, the one in the picture."

"No," Eleanor Quake said, shaking her head again. "They did check on that. They're not his prints."

Kelly smacked his fist into his other hand and swore. There went his best hope.

"If we could get a deep search done, there might still be a chance," Eleanor Quake offered with a half-hearted shrug. "But I don't think we have time. The FBI agent put me off."

"What's his name?" Kelly's father said. "I'll take care of it."

As Eleanor Quake responded, something nagged at Kelly. It was his recollection of the last time he'd had the pager. He struggled to recall it and the episode replayed on his mental TV screen. Fists of ice began to squeeze his vital organs. It was unthinkable. But other things said it was possible. He was desperate.

"Dad," he said, holding two envelopes out to his father. "Have them see if they can get any fingerprints besides mine off these. If they can, have 'em try matching them to the ones found on the pager and other stuff."

Eleanor Quake looked at the envelopes, then raised her eyes. "And if they match?"

"They probably won't," he said. "If they do…" He resigned himself. "If they do, I'll know who the missing robber is."

Thirty

Judge Velma Blackwell silently chopped the rim of her bench with stiff hands, frequently looking at the clock on the wall, then at Kelly.

At last Eleanor Quake pushed through the courtroom door, followed by Kelly's father. Quake hurried to her place at the defendant's table. "I apologize, Your Honor," she said. "May I have just a few moments with my client?"

The judge looked at the clock. "Tempus fugit, Ms. Quake. Make it brief."

"Thank you, Your Honor." Eleanor Quake dropped into her chair and motioned for Kelly to lean close to her, away from the other defendants. "You did it," she whispered nasally. "They matched prints off one of the papers you gave your father to the one from the pager. Then they ran it through a whole series of computer files. Found a match with a missing person—a girl named Maxine Burkhardt who disappeared from her home in Chicago when she was twelve. She'd be nearly eighteen now."

Kelly struggled to absorb this news as Eleanor Quake watched him closely. Maxine Burkhardt? How could that be?

Slowly he straightened up in his chair, then leaned in the other direction and whispered to Wasser, "Tink, did Amy ever tell you she used to live in Chicago?"

A smug expression appeared on Wasser's face. "You finally starting to wise up?" he said in a low voice. "Yeah, she came from Chicago. Ran away from her nigger stepfather when she was eleven or twelve. Her real name's not even Amy, and that so-called uncle she lives with is some long-haul truck driver who picked her up on the road."

Kelly stared blankly at the smirking Wasser. He wanted to call him a liar. He wanted to punch his lights out.

"You're such a sap," Wasser continued. "Amy belongs to X-Ray. She always has. Once in a while, he slaps her around and she collects some sucker like you." His facial expression changed to bitterness. "Or me. But she always goes back to him."

Stunned and hurt, Kelly tried to swallow, but couldn't. He had feared the worst…he thought. But this was beyond imagining.

Eleanor Quake's muted voice came unexpectedly. "She's visited X-Ray at the jail."

"Amy told me about that," Kelly said. "She went once to try and talk him into helping me."

"She's seen him two or three times a week ever since he's been in jail," Eleanor Quake said gently.

Kelly looked at her in helpless silence. Eleanor Quake, he thought, the lady who finds things you don't even know are lost.

Thirty-One

It was after 11:00 when the judge finally had the jury take their places the following morning. So much had happened since the prior day, Kelly sat exhausted in his place at the defendants' table.

"Let the record show—" Judge Blackwell rumbled through her routine opening, then faced the jury. "Ladies and gentlemen, additional evidence has been brought to the attention of the court. Counsels for the defense and the district attorney's office have agreed that this evidence materially affects this case in only one regard." She turned from the jury to the counselors. "The court will entertain a motion. Mr. Sanchez?"

"Your Honor," he said getting to his feet, "the people move to dismiss the charges against Francis Kelly."

Gasps and murmurs erupted from the spectators, and every eye in the room snapped to Kelly.

"The charges against Francis Kelly are dismissed," said Judge Blackwell, striking her gavel. "There will be a ten-minute recess, then court will reconvene and we will continue the case against the remaining defendants."

Chaos followed the judge's exit. Voices clamored for the district attorney and Kelly as the deputy sheriffs hustled X-Ray and Bubba out and Bailiff Woznowski cleared a path for the jurors through the crowd. Eleanor Quake took Kelly by the arm and began to lead him to the opening in the mid-court rail, but as they pressed through the people surrounding District Attorney Sanchez, Kelly stopped to listen.

"The new evidence we turned up," Sanchez was saying, "led to another suspect who was arrested and booked last night. The suspect is a minor and the name will not be released until we go to trial. It will be a separate trial."

"What was the evidence?" asked a hawk-nosed woman holding a microphone.

"You'll have to wait until the trial for that," Sanchez said. "But I can tell you this, it proves that the fourth robber in the van was the person we arrested last night and not Kelly."

So they had matched Amy's fingerprints to the ones found in the van as well as on the pager.

Eleanor Quake pulled at his arm. "Let's get out of here," she said.

"Mr. Kelly," the hawk-nosed woman said, following them up the aisle. "Could I have your reaction, Frank?"

That was a fatal mistake, lady, Kelly said to himself. Never call me Frank. He stepped into the corridor and followed Eleanor Quake toward his father, Bear, and Sharmin, who were waiting.

"Just a word or two," the woman persisted, tagging after him. She held her microphone out to him as they joined Bear and the others. "How do you feel—"

Bear pushed between Kelly and the woman. "He feels like taking a leak," he said. Then he shoved Kelly ahead of him into the men's restroom.

"Thanks, Bear," said Kelly, sighing with relief. "Let's cool it in here until that obnoxious woman finds somebody else to bother."

Kelly's father stuck his head inside the door. "We'll wait for you downstairs," he said with a smile, then closed the door.

For a moment they stood in silence. "How *do* you feel?" Bear said.

Kelly hesitated. "Terrible," he said finally.

"Amy?"

Kelly nodded. "It hurts, blood brother. You were right about her, but it still hurts."

Bear folded his arms and leaned back against a sink. "You'll find another," he said.

Kelly looked at himself in the mirror over the sinks. "I don't believe I'll be playing basketball this year," he said. "Do you think I could make the football team again?"

Thirty-Two

The air on the terrace outside the courthouse felt cool for a change. As they walked down the steps towards the pool with its spraying plumes of water, Kelly remembered Amy waiting there the first day of the trial. Now he saw his father standing with Eleanor Quake and Sharmin. His father looked up, then led the others to meet them.

"Dad," Kelly said quickly, "I want to thank you for—"

"I was just the expediter, son. Thank her." He nodded to Eleanor Quake.

Memories of his earlier behavior toward the attorney flashed through Kelly's mind as turned to her. "You were great miz Quake. And…you helped me see that the system works after all. Thank you."

His father put his arm around Kelly and gave him a manly squeeze. "I'm going to have to leave, son," he said. "I've got a plane to catch." He shook hands with each of the others. "You folks should all go celebrate." He parted with a wave.

Kelly echoed his father, his mind in a fog, "Yeah, celebrate."

Sharmin's voice interrupted his thoughts. "You should see this, Francis—I mean, Kelly." She held out a folded newspaper and pointed to a particular article. The headline said: "Teens On The Street." Below that were the words: "by Magnus Reid."

"Well, I'll be." muttered Kelley in amazement.

"You made a difference," Sharmin said.

Kelly tried to read the article, but he couldn't concentrate. Then he suddenly thought again of his father's parting words. He faced the others and said, "We do need to celebrate. We'll have a real blowout. I'll ask Soo Ling to whip up one of his eleven-course spectaculars, and you're all invited." He looked at Eleanor Quake, then placed one hand on Bear's shoulder, the other on Sharmin's.

Sharmin shook her head and looked disappointed. "Tonight's the rally."

"We're going down to the capitol," Bear said.

"Why don't we all go?" Eleanor Quake said, watching Kelly.

He waited a few seconds. "All right," he said. "I'll try being part of a solution." He looked at Sharmin and cocked his head. "But just this once. After that…after that, we'll see."

Sharmin broke into a wide smile, her big, dark eyes sparkling.

She's not bad to look at, he thought. Not bad at all.

FOR ADDITIONAL COPIES OF THIS BOOK, ask about "Print On Demand" publications at major bookstores. The Ingram "books in print" data base which contains this book is available at more than 25,000 retail outlets in the United States and around the world, including Barnes and Noble, Borders, and Amazon.

The Print On Demand system enables you to purchase books that may not be found on the dealer's shelves. You will need to know the exact title or author's name.

Print On Demand books may also be ordered via the internet. Visit: http://www.iUniverse.com for electronic or printed copies of "All Rise."

9 780595 091515